THE GATEWAY

© Copyright

PIERRE M. DROLET

ARCHWAY
PUBLISHING

Archway Publishing books may be ordered
through booksellers or by contacting:

Archway Publishing
1663 Liberty Drive
Bloomington, IN 47403
www.archwaypublishing.com
1-(888)-242-5904

Because of the dynamic nature of the Internet, any web addresses or
links contained in this book may have changed since publication and
may no longer be valid. The views expressed in this work are solely those
of the author and do not necessarily reflect the views of the publisher,
and the publisher hereby disclaims any responsibility for them.

Any people depicted in stock imagery provided by Thinkstock are
models, and such images are being used for illustrative purposes only.
Certain stock imagery © Thinkstock.

ISBN: 978-1-4808-0710-5 (sc)
ISBN: 978-1-4808-0711-2 (e)

Library of Congress Control Number: 2014906879

Printed in the United States of America

Archway Publishing rev. date: 04/10/2014

"If you want to find the secrets of the universe, think in terms of energy, frequency, and vibration."

—**Nikola Tesla**

Acknowledgments

I would like to give special thanks to the people who helped me realize this book project. As a CGI (computer-generated imagery) visual effects artist, I never would have imagined that one day I would write a book. English is my second language, and I have to admit that this issue was quite a challenge throughout the writing process.

The person I would like to thank first and foremost is my wonderful, beloved Lan Kao. With her kindness and generosity, she gave her time to perform the initial editing. She has been supportive of my writing project and beyond. Secondly, I would like to thank Joy M. for the final editing. And finally, many thanks to the talented artist Jesse Toves who created some of the initial illustrations in graphic novel style, which, unfortunately, are not included in the book.

Prologue

New York City, November 1944
11:11 p.m.

WHEN LOOKING AT THE CROWD walking peacefully through Times Square enjoying the nightlife, it's hard to believe that the United States is at war. The reality is different for a military unit stepping out of The Copa nightclub. This is the last night before they deploy to Europe from Mitchel Air Force Base located on the Hempstead Plains of Long Island.

One of the young soldiers in the group stops and looks up at the large, illuminated billboards and buildings around him. He is a bit drunk and starts feeling nostalgic about his hometown. "God, I'm gonna miss this," he says to himself. Shortly after he drifts off in his thoughts, two beautiful women passing by capture his attention, and one of them looks at him and smiles. He smiles back at her and says, "I'm gonna miss her too. I think I'm in love."

As the soldier stares at the beautiful woman walking away, he suddenly hears a crashing sonic boom in the sky that shocks him and everyone else in sight. "What the hell?" he exclaims.

An eerie silence follows as the crowd in the street is stunned by what has just happened. All eyes frantically look up in the sky. A few seconds pass before air-raid sirens sound off and searchlights illuminate the sky over the city. Peeking in and out through the clouds with incredible speed is a fireball that's heading straight for the city.

The drunken soldier can't believe what he sees and immediately yells, "We're under attack!"

Everybody runs for cover, panic-stricken as chaos erupts in the streets. As the fireball gets closer and closer, its trajectory suddenly shifts, and it begins a level flight just over the tallest buildings. The shockwave created by the fireball shatters windows, and glass shards rain on the crowded streets.

Gradually losing altitude, the fireball continues flying at high speeds above the city for many miles until it appears the unimaginable is about to happen. When it reaches the harbor, the fireball continues flying over the Hudson River in a collision course with the Statue of Liberty. The impact seems imminent until the fireball comes to a dead stop one hundred feet from Lady Liberty's face. The fireball dissipates, and a strange, saucer-shaped aircraft appears. Still smoking, the brownish metallic aircraft is sixty feet in diameter and looks like a squashed bell. The aircraft silently hovers and wobbles as it defies gravity.

Three miles away, two Curtiss P-40 fighter planes are flying in the area to intercept the uninvited UFO. As they approach, both pilots stare in disbelief.

"What in the hell is that?" the lieutenant exclaims, speaking into his headset microphone.

"I don't know, but it's definitely not one of ours." The captain changes the radio channel. "Control tower, this is Tiger One. I have visual contact on one foo fighter, possibly hostile. Request authorization to open fire."

"Authorization granted, Tiger One," the control tower operator says through heavy static interference.

The captain changes course and engages the aircraft. "Roger that."

As soon as his crosshairs lock on to the target,

the captain opens fire. A trail of lead hits the enemy aircraft with unexpected results. Very little damage seems to be inflicted on the UFO; it's as if the bullets decelerate drastically a few inches from the aircraft before bouncing off the surface. Both pilots are puzzled at this first attack, and the lieutenant is clearly worried.

"We're gonna need bigger guns," he calls out.

The aircraft starts to move slowly in a clumsy, wobbling manner.

"Maybe not," the captain says, looking on as the foo fighter appears to be struggling. "Here's our chance to finish it."

Both P-40s engage the target for a second attack and open fire again. The result appears to be the same, as the bullets bounce off the surface of the UFO, but this time, the craft makes an evasive maneuver before accelerating to an incredible speed and disappearing.

"Holy shit! Did you see that?" the lieutenant cries out.

"Yeah, but I wish I hadn't." The captain changes the radio channel one more time. "Control tower, this is Tiger One. Can you see the foo fighter on your radar?"

The pilot hears a few seconds of static noise in his headphones before the control tower responds. "Negative, Tiger One," the man from the control tower replies.

"Whatever it was, it's now gone." The captain concludes.

Both P-40s break the pursuit and return to the base.

Chapter 1

**Present Day, 33,000 Feet over the Pacific Ocean
5:26 p.m.**

Two AV-8B Harrier jump jets flying in formation are
on their way to the Marine Corps Air Station Miramar
in San Diego. Maj. Matthew Schauberger and his
wingman, Capt. Daniel Myers, are coming back from
a six-month tour of duty in the Middle East. Both
are good-looking men in their early thirties who are
physically fit and ruggedly charming. They have known
each other for nine years and are good friends. Today
is an uneasy day for both of them, because this is the
last time they will fly together. Matt is retiring from the
Marine Corps.

Daniel, in his mischievous way, takes this last
opportunity to try and convince his friend to change
his mind. "Come on, Matt, admit it—you're gonna miss
flying with me."

In a quick move, Daniel rolls his Harrier jump jet over the top of Matt's AV-8B and ends up on the other side, just a few feet from the wingtip. Matt smiles and shakes his head in amusement of Daniel's relentless persistence.

"Show-off!" Matt calls out. "Is that all you've got?"

Daniel stabilizes his Harrier. "Are you sure you want to give up all of this?"

Matt reflects on his decision to retire from the military and has no regrets. "I served my country for ten years. I think it's time for me to move on and eventually start a family."

"Too bad you won't be around for the new F-35," Daniel says.

Matt knocks gently on the dashboard of his Harrier. "Yeah. I'm not the only one who's retiring."

"Well, personally, I can't see myself doing anything

else other than flying for a living," Daniel adds sarcastically. "What are you going to do if you're not flying? Get fat and play golf?"

"C'mon, man!" Matt jokingly yells out in his own defense. "You know I have more options than that. Actually, I've been getting e-mails from the company my dad used to work for."

The news surprises Daniel. He knew Matt's father had worked as a researcher for a technology corporation. "That's interesting. I thought your dad was a scientist."

"He was, but he also had an engineering background like me."

At a young age, Matt showed signs of being a gifted child. He grew up with the privilege of being part of an advanced education program and went on to graduate from MIT with a degree in electrical engineering prior to turning twenty. After graduation, he made the bold decision to join the military, which was motivated by his taste for adventure and new challenges. He turned away from a promising career in engineering and thereby changed his destiny.

Daniel is curious and wants to know more. "So, what are those e-mails about?"

"They asked me to contact them when I get back," Matt answers.

Daniel immediately jumps to the obvious conclusion. "Hey, maybe they want to offer you a job."

Matt thinks about it for a moment. "I don't know about that, and even if that's the case, I'm in no rush. If I start a new job right away, Kayla is not going to be happy with me. I promised her that we would take some time off together."

Kayla is Matt's fiancé and have experienced their share of ups and downs throughout their long-distance relationship over the past few years. Daniel chuckles and cannot resist the chance to mess with his friend. "Well, I'm actually not worried about you. I just feel bad for Kayla, because she's the one who's going to have to deal with having you around the house all the time."

Matt rolls his eyes and smiles. "You're an ass."

"I know." Daniel takes a deep breath and adds, "I need a hug."

"Nah ... you need to get laid. Get off my back for a second and look ahead."

Still far away on the horizon, Matt is looking through the haze hovering over the Southern California coast. "Home sweet home," Matt says as he gazes at the horizon, anticipating his homecoming.

They start their descent for the approach at Air Station Miramar.

A few miles away, before they land, the control tower operator contacts Matt and Daniel. "Tower One to VMA-501 and 504; runway 24R is cleared for landing. Welcome home, boys."

"Roger. Good to be back, Tower One," Matt says.

Both AV-8B Harriers touch down on the runway and taxi their jump jets at the end of a row, where other Marines and Navy fighter jets are already parked.

Inside a nearby building, a beautiful brunette in her late twenties named Kayla Masson is looking out the window, waiting anxiously for the arrival of her beloved Matt.

Twenty-five minutes later, both pilots walk to the flight arrival area with their backpacks. Kayla runs to Matt and gives him a big, long hug. They gaze at each other for a moment in disbelief. They are finally reunited. He gently pulls his sweetheart closer for a tender kiss.

"I've missed you," Kayla says with her sweet voice.

Matt kisses her again before he replies, "I've missed you too, babe—more than you know."

Kayla lets go of Matt and looks at Daniel who is waiting with open arms. "Come here, beautiful," he says. "I need some love too."

Kayla reaches out and gives him a hug. "It's good to see you, Danny."

Matt grabs Daniel's shoulder. "Are you sure you don't need a ride to LA?"

"No, I'm good, thanks. I'm going to stay with my folks down here for a few days," Daniel says.

Matt hugs his friend before leaving the air station. "All right, buddy. I'll see you later."

Brentwood, Los Angeles

AFTER A THREE-HOUR DRIVE UP north along the Southern California coast in his SUV, Matt pulls in to the driveway of his house. Kayla and Matt are finally home. The house is cozy and located in the trendy, upscale neighborhood of Brentwood. When Matt's family first moved to Brentwood in the late 1970s, it was just another suburban neighborhood like most other middle-class areas at the time. Matt was lucky to inherit the house from his father, Cedric Schauberger; otherwise, he never would have been able to afford such a home on a pilot's salary.

Matt opens the front door and drops his backpack on the floor near the entryway. He walks inside and stops in front of the fireplace. A framed Tibetan mandala painting is hanging on the wall, and below there are multiple photos of him and Kayla. There are also a few pictures of his family, including an old photo of his late mother who died in a car accident only three months after Matt's first birthday. He then looks over at one of his favorite pictures of his father and him when he was just ten years old. They are both standing in front of a single-engine light airplane, a Piper PA-28 Cherokee. Matt used to love flying with his dad on weekends. Reminiscing over the family photos, he starts to feel sad but contains his emotions and quietly says to himself. "I'm home, Dad."

Kayla sneaks up behind him and gives him a hug. Matt is still staring at his father in the pictures and shares his regret with Kayla. "I didn't get the chance to say good-bye."

—————

Indian Ocean, Amphibious Assault Ship *USS Wasp* A Year Earlier

MATT IS CLIMBING DOWN FROM his AV-8B Harrier. An officer comes to meet him on the flight deck. "Sir! Captain Thompson wants to see you in his office."

Matt knows it is usually bad news when the captain of the ship asks to see a pilot in his office. The captain's request puts Matt in an edgy state, and as he proceeds to walk to the office, his gut starts to feel heavy with nervousness. Nothing could have prepared him for what he was about to hear. The pilot enters the office, stands at attention, and salutes Captain Thompson.

"At ease, Major Schauberger. Please have a seat," the captain says with a firm voice.

"Thank you, sir," Matt replies.

The captain seems anxious and looks at Matt for a moment before he speaks. "I have some bad news for you. I was just informed that your father, Cedric Schauberger, was in a plane accident ... The report says no survivors were found at the crash site."

Matt has a hard time processing what he has just heard. His first reaction is denial. "Are you sure you have the right Cedric Schauberger?" he asks in complete disbelief.

Captain Thompson replies, "Yes, the body was identified and confirmed two days ago."

Like a good marine, Matt stays calm and shows no emotional reaction in front of his superior officer. Captain Thompson looks at Matt and, with a sincere tone of voice, expresses his sympathy. "I am truly sorry for your loss."

Cedric had raised Matt as a single parent and was his only family. Grief rushes through Matt's body, and his eyes start watering. While he is fighting to keep in his emotions, the pilot decides that it would be a good time to leave the office before any tears come out.

"Thank you for taking the time—" Matt takes a deep breath, but no words come out. He cannot finish his sentence. He stands tall and adds, "Will that be all, sir?"

He takes the captain by surprise. "Yes … that is all."

Matt salutes Captain Thompson and exits the office. As soon as the door closes behind him, the marine closes his eyes to catch his breath. He is overwhelmed by the multitude of emotions, and all he can do is to let the tears flow down his face.

Kayla is looking at a picture of Matt's father. "He would have been proud of you," she says.

Matt isn't so sure. "You should have seen the look on his face when I told him I was going to join the military."

Cedric had always wanted Matt to follow in his footsteps, for him to become a scientist, but Kayla never knew that. It had been a big disappointment for Cedric to see Matt join the Marine Corps.

"Well, I am certainly proud of you," Kayla says with her sweet voice.

Matt turns around to face Kayla and kisses her passionately. He reaches down for her legs and sweeps her up. Matt carries Kayla upstairs to the bedroom and gently lays her down on the bed. They slowly undress each other while softly kissing and then passionately make love.

Chapter 2

THE NEXT MORNING, MATT IS quietly eating his breakfast at the kitchen counter. Kayla is dressed and ready to leave for work. She is a lawyer in a downtown LA firm. "I'm late for work," Kayla says with hurry in her voice as she grabs Matt's face and gives him a kiss. "Enjoy your time off. Love you!"

Matt smiles at her. "Love you too."

Kayla rushes out of the house, and Matt watches her leave. He takes a few more bites of his cereal and looks around, lost in his thoughts. The peaceful quietness of the house suddenly makes Matt feel uneasy. Right then, he misses the sound of a jet engine and the wind blowing on the flight deck. In that moment, reality hits him—he may never hear those sweet sounds again.

Matt grabs his leather jacket and goes to the garage. He presses the control, and the garage door opens. An overloaded storage shelf is stacked with boxes, all labeled with his father's name. The boxes take up more than a third of the garage space. Next to the empty parking space are two motorcycles covered with weather cloths. He takes the dusty motorcycle cover off of one of them and reveals a black BMW K1200R. Matt takes his full-face helmet from the storage shelf and gets on his bike, ready for a ride.

Matt starts the engine, and as he rides down his driveway, a black Mercedes-Benz limousine pulls up at the same time and blocks him. The driver steps out and opens the back door of the limo. He looks at Matt and, with a firm voice, says to him, "Mr. Waizer would like to see you."

Matt takes off his helmet, a bit upset, and walks

toward the limo. He gets in, and the driver closes the door behind him. A charismatic, very old man in an expensive suit is sitting in the limo. It's none other than Herbert Waizer. He is the CEO of WTRD, Waizer Technology Research and Development Corporation.

There is a flat-screen TV on the ceiling of the limo. CNN is on showing coverage of the presidential campaign, and the anchorman talks about the two candidates: Sen. Karl Waizer, who happens to be Herbert Waizer's son, and Andrew Cooper.

Herbert engages Matt in German. "How are you, Son? It's been a long time since we've seen each other."

Herbert gives Matt a stiff hug. Matt speaks German fluently and answers him in the same language. "Mr. Waizer, I'm doing well, thank you. Sir, why are you here?"

"You didn't answer my e-mails, and I was in the neighborhood, so I thought I would stop by," Herbert says, looking straight at him with a sneering smile.

Matt doesn't have any excuse, except that he never really liked the old man. Matt has known him all his life, and even as a child, he always found Herbert's presence intimidating. "I just got back yesterday. How did you know I was back?"

"I have my sources." Herbert switches back to English. "Your German is impeccable—no accent at all."

"I grew up with Dad speaking mostly German at

home, and I was stationed two years in Germany …
That sure helped," Matt says.

Herbert looks at the house through the car window.
"I miss your father … Cedric was a loyal friend and the
most valuable member of the company."

Cedric's plane crash had happened a year earlier in
a Herbert Waizer corporate jet, and Matt still couldn't
help associating the death of his dad with the old man.
Matt uses the election to change the subject. On TV,
he sees Karl Waizer shaking hands with people in the
crowd.

"Do you think Karl has a good chance to beat
Cooper?" Matt asks.

"Yes, my son is a better candidate than Cooper, and
he is destined to be president," the proud father says.

Matt scratches his head. "A man like you doesn't
just happen to be in the neighborhood. Why are you
really here?"

"All right … it's about your father's legacy,"
Herbert says.

This takes Matt by surprise and also hits a nerve.
"What about it?"

"The official report says Cedric's death was a plane
crash, but there is more to it than that."

Matt is all ears. "What do you mean?"

Herbert leans forward. "The cause of his death is
highly classified because of the implication of his work."

Hearing this information upsets Matt. "Why are you telling me this now?"

Herbert looks down. "Out of respect for Cedric, I need to come clean with you."

Matt is growing impatient. "What happened to him?" he demands.

The old man remains silent for a moment. "Listen, why don't you stop by my office tomorrow? I'll explain everything."

"What?! Wait a second! You're telling me there is a cover-up with my dad's death. I want answers now!"

With a calm voice, Herbert replies, "Please, just hear me out. I want to make things right, but a simple explanation will not be enough. I also want to show you something. Trust me—you will not be disappointed." The old man smiles at him. "I will see you tomorrow morning."

Matt stares at him briefly with trepidation and nods before getting out. As he watches the limousine leave, he can't help but be disturbed about what he has just heard.

Later in the evening, Kayla comes home from work and parks the SUV in the garage. She gets out and holds the overloaded storage shelf for balance to take off her shoes. Kayla hears a crackling noise, which sounds like the shelf is about to break. She lets go of the shelf and looks at it, expecting it to fall apart any second. Fortunately, the shelf holds.

Inside the house, Matt is sitting on the couch in the living room. He is watching the news on the flat-screen television.

The anchorman reports, "The polls show a tight race between Karl Waizer and Andrew Cooper, but Cooper seem to have a slight lead in the votes."

Kayla arrives in the living room and falls on the couch beside Matt. "Hi, honey!" She kisses him.

"Hi, babe!" he answers back.

Matt moves closer to her as Kayla lays her head down on her lover's shoulder. "You should do something with all of your dad's boxes in the garage. I think that shelf is on its last leg."

"I'll add it to my to-do list," Matt says with a smile.

Kayla feels relaxed and enjoys this moment with her beloved. "How was your day?" she asks.

Matt has to think about it for a moment. "Kind of strange."

Kayla shows surprise. "What do you mean?"

"I got a visit from Herbert Waizer himself."

"Waizer? Why does that name sound familiar?"

Matt points to the flat-screen TV where Karl Waizer is making a speech. "His name sounds familiar because he is that guy's father and the CEO of Waizer

Technology Research and Development … He used to be my dad's boss."

Kayla has no reason to be concerned, but she senses that something is not quite right. "What does he want with you? Did he offer you a job?"

"He didn't say anything about a job. He wants me to stop by his office tomorrow," Matt says.

Kayla is not satisfied with his answer and feels there is something more to this visit. "You don't sound too excited about it. Is there more to this than you are telling me?"

Matt doesn't want to go into greater detail about his unexpected visit without knowing more from Herbert, and he doesn't want Kayla to worry about it. "No, babe. Waizer just caught me by surprise when he showed up out of nowhere. Seeing him brought back some bad memories." Matt avoids looking in her eyes and seems preoccupied.

"I know that face." Kayla knows he'll talk when he's ready, but that doesn't stop her from trying to get a little more information. "Honey, you know I'm here for you … right?"

"I know." Matt takes a deep breath. "Listen, it's something personal between me and Waizer. Until I know more, I prefer to deal with it by myself."

"Okay, have it your way. I know it's hard for you to open up, but in the future, no more secrets.

Hopefully, you'll tell me what's going on in that head of yours; otherwise, I'm going to have to kick your ass. Understood, soldier?" Kayla makes a funny face and starts tickling Matt's rib cage.

"Yes, ma'am," Matt says as he salutes her.

"I'm serious! Are you going to at least try?"

"Yes, master! I mean, ma'am." Matt is tickling Kayla back, and they both fall on the couch laughing.

Chapter 3

IT IS ANOTHER BEAUTIFUL, SUNNY day in Los Angeles. Matt is riding his motorcycle on the 405 Freeway, cutting through traffic as he heads to the Waizer Corporation located in Northridge. He is a bit tired this morning, as he hadn't been able to sleep the night before. He had been anxiously anticipating meeting with Herbert Waizer and learning what the old man knew about his father's death.

About twenty minutes later, Matt arrives at his destination. On the front yard of the gated establishment, an unmistakable imposing block of concrete is standing with the steel engraving: WTRD. Even though it is not obvious at first sight, the perimeter is monitored 24/7 with the latest technology in security. There are several industrial buildings on site, and before Matt can access the area, he stops at the main gate for a security check. One of the two armed security guards comes out of the gatehouse to meet him.

"Good morning," the guard says. "What is your business here?"

Matt pulls his driver's license out of his jacket pocket and shows it to the security guard. "My name is Matthew Schauberger. I have a meeting with Mr. Herbert Waizer."

The guard looks at Matt for a second. "Wait here." The security guard walks back to the gatehouse and makes a phone call. After a few minutes of security checks, the guard comes back with a guest pass and gives it to Matt. "Mr. Waizer's office is in the next building on the right," the guard says as he points his finger in the direction of the building.

"Thank you," Matt replies. He had come here many times in the past to meet his father and was familiar with the area.

After parking his motorcycle, Matt takes the elevator to the penthouse of the twenty-one-floor building. As soon as he gets out of the elevator, a beautiful blonde woman in her midthirties walks up to greet him. "Mr. Schauberger?"

"Yes," Matt replies.

"Hi, I'm Rachel, Mr. Waizer's personal assistant. Please follow me. I will take you to his office." The woman smiles at Matt and starts to walk away.

"Thank you," Matt says before turning to follow her.

When they arrive at the office, Rachel politely steps aside of the open door and says, "After you."

As Matt steps in Waizer's office, Rachel closes the door behind him. The office looks more like a small museum than a workplace, with various extravagant art collections, artifacts, paintings, and statues. Herbert is sitting behind a massive wooden desk. "I'm glad you came, Matthew. Please have a seat."

"Thank you, sir."

Herbert stares at Matt for a moment. "Before we go any further, I want to remind you that everything we will talk about today is highly classified and a matter of national security. Are we clear about this?"

"Yes, sir," Matt agrees. "You have my word."

This is not the first time Matt had dealt with national security issues. Having been in the Marine Corps, he knew the drill.

"Very well," Herbert says. He stands up from his chair and walks toward the exit door. "Come with me. I want to show you something."

After sitting down for just about a minute, Matt stands up and leaves the office with the mysterious old man.

Ten minutes later, they access another building and walk down a corridor. "Officially, this section of the facility doesn't exist. Very few people have access and only a handful of people have the privilege to know its secret," Herbert says.

The corridor leads to a big stainless-steel door, the kind of vault door you would expect to see in a highly secure bank, not in a building research establishment. Herbert pulls an ID card from his vest pocket.

"Please step aside," he directs.

Matt moves a few feet away while Herbert swipes his ID card and enters a security code. Multiple green lasers scan Herbert's full body, and lock mechanism sounds can be heard. The door opens automatically, and they both step into the dark room. The door closes behind them, and lights turn on, revealing a high-tech laboratory that is the size of a small warehouse.

In the middle of the lab, two unusual Tesla coil motors stand facing each other. Each one is about twelve feet in diameter, and they stand about ten feet apart. They are spinning in opposite directions at a slow RPM. Electric spark discharges are flowing between the Tesla coils, forming arcs, and loud crackling noise can be heard. "Your father left behind one of the greatest contributions to science," the old man says.

Matt passes by a worn-out yellow duct tape X marked on the floor. At first sight, the lab looks like a sophisticated powerhouse with heavy-duty electrical cables hanging all over the place. Several power supply generators are aligned on the wall and a workstation on a mezzanine. Matt is impressed by what he sees but still doesn't know what it is used for.

"That's a hell of a power plant for one lab! What are you trying to accomplish here?" Matt questions.

Herbert looks at the high-tech gears surrounding him before answering the question. "The impossible."

Matt follows the old man to the main control area and turns on a few switches. The two giant Tesla coils start to spin faster and faster. Suddenly, they hear eerie, high-pitched sounds and crackling noises, and electric sparks rapidly intensify.

"This lab runs completely on self-generated power, separate from the rest of the company. It's your father's design." Herbert walks over to one of the computers, types a code on the keyboard, and presses Enter. He then pushes a rolling office chair to Matt. "Take it with you."

The old man also takes an office chair with him and uses it like a rolling walker as he pushes it toward the two giant Tesla coils. He stops about fifteen feet away from the coils. At this point, Matt begins to feel apprehensive about the wind generated by the coils' high RPM and loud noise.

"Sir! I don't think we should get any closer to that thing!" he warns.

Mesmerized, Herbert just stares at the fierce electromagnetic storm created between the two giant Tesla coils. "Your father named it The Gateway."

Herbert slowly pushes the rolling office chair in between the two Tesla coils. When the chair hits the electromagnetic storm, aka The Gateway, it violently bounces back, flies straight into the air, and then breaks apart on the wall.

Matt ducks. "Jesus Christ! Why did you do that?"

The old man looks at him like nothing happened. He takes away Matt's chair and lifts it in his arms.

"Ah! C'mon now, sir!" Matt pleads. "Please put the chair down!"

Herbert smirks at him before swinging the chair around his body as hard as he can and then throwing it straight into the gateway. Matt gets down again, expecting to see the chair flying again in the air like a projectile.

"Shit!" he yells.

This time, the chair does not bounce back. It doesn't

pass through the other side of the gateway either. It just vanishes in to thin air. As soon as the chair disappears, the gateway collapses on itself like an implosion. The power source in the entire lab then shuts down for a few seconds, creating total darkness and silence. When the lights come on, Matt has a hard time processing what he'd just seen.

"What happened to the chair?" he asks.

Herbert stares at the gateway for a few seconds. "Yeah, that's the million-dollar question. Your father knew how to bring objects back from the gateway. Since he's been gone, we haven't been able to repeat the experiment."

Matt starts to make some connections. "When you told me there was more to my dad's death, were you referring to this?"

"Yes," Herbert answers.

"Is this what happened to my dad?" Matt walks towards the two giant Tesla coils to have a closer look.

"I'm afraid so. He put himself through the gateway to test it, but he never came back."

"Is he really dead? Or—" Matt asks out of desperation.

"I don't know. Cedric found a way to open a door to another dimension." Herbert walks back to the main control area and turns off all the switches.

"Another dimension?" This is mind-boggling for

Matt. "There is a chance that he could be trapped in there."

"That is one of the possibility," Herbert agrees.

"Is there a way to bring him back?"

Herbert grabs Matt by his shoulder. "This is why I brought you here."

Matt looks around the lab again, but this time an uneasy feeling of intimidation takes over his mind. "I know he was working on some kind of quantum theory project … but that is something else."

"You are more than a gifted fighter pilot," the old man says. "You also have a PhD in electrical engineering. I want to give you a chance to follow in your father's footsteps and finish his lifetime work."

Herbert knew too well that it was Cedric's dream to work with his son in the same laboratory. For the first time in ten years, Matt begins to regret his decision to join the military. A feeling of guilt is growing inside him for not being there for his father. He is convincing himself that he is somehow responsible for what happened to his single parent.

"I wasn't aware this technology even existed. Where am I supposed to start with all this?"

Herbert opens a storage cabinet. "Thanks to your father, it was possible to bring objects back from the gateway with this device."

Inside the cabinet there is a pile of burned, damaged,

and strange-looking devices the size of a soccer ball. Herbert takes one from the pile and gives it to Matt. "Each one of these devices is handmade. Each one made it back from the gateway once but was damaged beyond repair."

As Matt looks down at the object, he notes that the protective case is made out of carbon fiber. On top, there is a screen display about the size of a smartphone. Next to the screen is a half-shaped metal ball.

"How does this work?" Matt asks.

"Think of it as a very sophisticated GPS that allows you to travel through space and time anywhere you want, in the blink of an eye."

Matt stares at the device and looks around for a moment. It doesn't take him long to connect the dots. "This is some kind of a time machine, isn't it?" Herbert nods before Matt adds, "This is unbelievable! How the hell did my dad end up working on a time machine, and I didn't know anything about it?"

A little smirk appears on Herbert's face before he answers. "Son, your family history has been hidden from you for your own protection."

Matt is both annoyed and puzzled about the comment. "What are you talking about?" he questions.

Herbert comes closer to Matt. "You come from a bloodline of genius scientists, and this is the only thing you have to know. I am giving you the opportunity to complete your father's work … and hopefully, in the process, help us unlock the mystery of what happened to him in the gateway." Herbert puts his hand on Matt's shoulder. "It's up to you."

The old man walks away toward the exit door, giving Matt some space to process all the information he has just heard and the decision he has to make.

Brentwood, Los Angeles

AFTER THE MEETING WITH WAIZER, Matt goes for a motorcycle ride in the Malibu Hills for the rest of the day to clear his head. Late in the evening, he arrives at home. By now, he's already made his decision about the old man's offer, but the hardest part is yet to come. He has to face Kayla with the news. He already knows she is not going to like what she hears, and he hasn't quite figured out how he will sell the idea without upsetting her.

Kayla is on the couch working on her iPad when Matt arrives from behind and kisses her neck.

"Where have you been?" she asks. "I've been trying to call you."

Matt retrieves his smartphone from his motorcycle jacket and sees the missed calls on the display. "Riding in the hills," he answers.

He sits down on the couch beside Kayla without saying anything. He is preoccupied with his thoughts, but it's time to face the music. Kayla looks at Matt, patiently waiting for him to say something. "So, how did your meeting go?"

Matt thinks for a second but decides to be straightforward. "Waizer offered me a job … and I'm starting Monday morning."

He takes her by surprise with this news. "Okay … so what kind of work are you going to be doing?"

Matt is uncomfortable. "I can't tell you. It's classified."

"What?!" Kayla wants to smile, but Matt looks at her with an honest, straight face. "You aren't joking, are you?"

Matt just shakes his head no without looking at her. Kayla is very disappointed and doesn't hide her feelings about it.

"Great. More secrets … just what we need in our relationship," she snaps back at him.

This is not the first time Matt has heard this one. For many years, Matt was not able to talk much about his work in the Marine Corps.

"C'mon! Give me a break," he says.

"I thought we were done dealing with all of this once you retired from the military," Kayla remarks, hoping that she might be able to convince him otherwise.

Matt is struggling to justify his decision without giving away too much information. "You don't understand. I *have* to take this job."

"You're right. I don't understand," she agrees. "You're the one who wanted to take some time off for us, and I thought it would be the perfect time to start our own—" Kayla stops herself before becoming too emotional. "Matthew, your dad left you a beautiful house and enough money to be financially secure for a long time. What is suddenly the rush for you to go back to work?"

Matt knows that she has all the reasons in the world to be angry with him. "Look, Waizer offered me a job, and I took the opportunity. What was I supposed to do? Just walk away?"

"That's not what I mean, but you could at least talk to me before you make a decision like this. I don't know what the deal is with Waizer, but I don't like the effect he has on you. Look at yourself," she says. "You are starting a new job, and instead of being excited, you look more like someone who just came back from a funeral. I want you to tell me what's really going on."

Pushed against the wall, Matt finally opens up. "The only thing I can tell you is that this job is very important to me because it has to do with continuing my dad's work."

Kayla calms down and takes a deep breath. "Your father was a scientist … That's all the information you gave me about his work, so I still don't know what you're new job is about. Moments like this make me worry about having a family with you. What is going to come first? Your work or your family?"

Kayla is disappointed by the way Matt had left her out of this important decision, and she leaves the living room very upset.

"Kayla!" Matt calls after her, but she doesn't respond.

She is already on her way to the bedroom and is ready to call it a night. Meanwhile, Matt struggles with his decision and the truth of what Kayla had said. He holds his head, angry with himself for the way he'd handled the situation.

Chapter 4

FOR THE ENTIRE WEEKEND, MATT was on his best behavior and tried to make up with Kayla for what he'd put her through. On Saturday morning, he surprised her with a bouquet of purple orchids and a card. He took her to San Onofre Beach, which was her favorite surf spot. He finished the weekend on a good note by taking her out to her favorite Italian restaurant. Even after all that, Matt knows he's only halfway out of the doghouse, but he's working on it.

Northridge, WTRD

IT'S MONDAY, AND AFTER ONLY one week since Matt is back from his tour of duty, he is starting his new job. Once he arrives at the Waizer Corporation, he is taken through all kinds of security protocols.

Later in the day, with his new ID card issued, the new recruit is free to walk around the industrial facility without any supervision. He heads toward the same building where he had been with Herbert the previous week.

When Matt arrives at his father's laboratory, he swipes his ID card and enters a security code. Multiple green lasers scan Matt's body, and lock mechanism sounds can be heard. The imposing stainless-steel vault door opens. He walks into the lab, and as he does, the door closes behind him. Matt looks around and doesn't see anyone else in the room.

"Hello!" he calls out.

An echo bounces back, but there is no answer. His new workplace is drastically different than the *USS Wasp*, the busy, amphibious assault ship where he had previously worked. Matt walks up the stairs to the mezzanine and sits down at the workstation. He turns on the computer and enters a password.

Herbert had given Matt full access to his late father's work regarding time travel. As soon as he accesses the network, hundreds of folders pop up on the computer screen.

"Here we go!" Matt says to himself as he opens a file from the first folder.

Matt's first month at the Waizer Corporation was one of the most challenging times of his life. The work was pretty intense and overwhelming, as he was trying to catch up the best he could with his father's lifetime of work. The science behind time travel is mind-boggling, but the rookie scientist knew he was up for the challenge, and in the process, he remains fascinated by everything he is learning.

After spending days reviewing the blueprints of the time machine device over and over again, Matt thinks he's finally ready to perform his first test experiment. His only objective right now is to make this high-tech gismo work and then use it to discover what had happened to his dad. On his work desk, a box with all the electronics and parts he needs for his first test have been prepared for him.

Using the blueprint as reference, Matt follows every step of the instruction. The time travel device begins taking shape. The most tedious part for Matt is to weld together the electronic components on the tiny circuit board. With the USB cable plugged in to the computer, Matt downloads the software program to the device and proceeds with the testing.

It takes him two weeks to complete his first device. Surprisingly, without the sphere carbon fiber protective case, it's only about the size of a smartphone.

When he is finally ready to test it, Matt takes the time travel device and positions himself thirty feet away from the giant Tesla coils. From where he stands, he enters the location coordinates on the touch screen. The interface is similar to a GPS device except for the additional time section. Matt looks at his wristwatch and enters a time into the device that is five minutes later than the current time. As he presses Enter on the touch screen, Matt looks down at his feet and realizes that he is standing on the yellow duct tape *X* marked on the floor.

"Oh … this is what those *X* marks are used for," he says to himself.

Matt begins walking back to the workstation to power up the giant Tesla coils. As he takes his position fifteen feet from both Tesla coils, they start spinning in opposite directions faster and faster. The wind generated by the Tesla coils' high RPM and the loud noise reminds him of the apprehensive feeling he'd felt the first time he saw them.

The Tesla coils are now reaching full power, and a fierce electromagnetic storm is forming between them.

Matt is swinging the time travel device back and forth, getting ready to throw it into the gateway.

"This is it!"

At that moment, Matt throws it hard, right in between the two Tesla coils. The time device vanishes in the gateway as it implodes with a sound of thunder. The electricity goes out for a few seconds and then comes back on. Matt turns his attention to the yellow duct tape X marked on the floor. He looks at his wristwatch and starts the countdown. The only thing he can do now is wait for the time device to reappear.

The last two minutes feel like forever, and according to his calculation, it should be back any second now.

Matt whispers a countdown under his breath. "Three … two … one!" Nothing happens.

With optimism, Matt waits for another hour to pass before he finally accepts that the time device is lost. Although he is disappointed by his first attempt, he doesn't waste any time getting back to work and preparing to build another time device.

Unfortunately, his next five attempts end with the same result as the first. On the sixth attempt, Matt throws the time device into the gateway but somehow doesn't throw it fast enough. It bounces back violently from the gateway and hits him in the stomach so hard that he falls in pain onto the floor. To add to the insult, an electric discharge from the gateway zaps Matt's metal wristwatch.

He quickly rips off his watch and throws it away. From that time on, he uses a plastic stopwatch instead.

On the ninth, tenth, and eleventh attempts, the time device just travels through the gateway and falls to the other side on the floor.

After six months of intensive work, a dozen trials, and failure to make the time device reappear, Matt is frustrated and decides to take a different approach. At this point, he is pretty convinced that something is wrong with the data he is using. If this is the case, he doesn't know how to fix it; however, he does know how to identify which data is broken by accessing the backdoor source code.

Running a program to scan and analyze the database, Matt is not surprise when he sees the results. After comparing dates of creation and code line mismatch, his suspicion is confirmed—he was working with an inadequate database. The rookie scientist is angry with himself for not performing this analysis prior to building the first time device. He decides that it is time to pay a visit to his boss.

Matt arrives at the front desk of Herbert Waizer's office and recognizes a familiar face. "Hi, I'm here to see Mr. Waizer," Matt says to Rachel, Waizer's personal assistant.

"Good morning, Mr. Schauberger. Mr. Waizer is ready to see you," Rachel replies while working at her computer. She smiles at him before standing up and escorting him to Herbert's office. "Please follow me."

"Thank you."

When they arrive, Rachel closes the office door behind Matt as he walks toward Herbert's desk.

"Please have a seat," Herbert says. The old man is busy with some administration paperwork as he addresses Matt.

"Thank you, sir." Matt sits down and stares at Herbert for a moment.

"Are you making any progress?" Waizer asks with anticipation.

Matt takes a deep breath before answering. "I'm working on it."

"Good … so, what is this urgent matter that you need to speak with me about?"

Matt hands Herbert a document with the source code analysis results from the database. "Something doesn't add up. I checked the source code for errors, and I found a lot of inconsistency between dates and code lines. It's like someone has been trying to fill in gaps with outdated data. That would explain why I've had no luck so far making the device reappear. My question is, how was Dad able to do it?"

Herbert looks at the document for a few seconds before slowly standing up and looking outside the window. "Cedric succeeded in traveling into the future, but something went terribly wrong when he attempted to go into the past. He didn't vanish quietly. The powerful energy released from the gateway overloaded and corrupted our network system, including his work. We recovered only fragments of it."

Matt is upset by this unexpected information. "Don't you guys keep any backup?"

"Your father was in charge of it. So far, we haven't been able to find anything in the system or in the database vault."

Matt feels like he has just wasted six months of his life. His hope to find his father suddenly vanishes, and he realized that in the process he might have jeopardized his relationship with Kayla. "I would have appreciated being told this earlier—before I started."

Herbert comes closer to Matt to make his appeal like an emotionally beat-up old man. "I was afraid you would have turned down my offer. You are the son of Cedric … If there is someone who can make it work, I think it's you. I am sorry, Matthew; I have not been entirely honest with you."

The rookie scientist bitterly stands up and looks straight in Herbert's eyes. "Yeah … I'm sorry too."

Ending the conversation with those last words, Matt leaves the office.

Chapter 5

IT HAS BEEN AWHILE SINCE the last time Kayla and Matt went surfing at San Onofre Beach. For the occasion, they invited Daniel to join them. Surfing for Matt is the perfect way to release some stress and remember what's important in life. The three friends are having fun in the ocean catching waves. However, after a few hours of surfing, Kayla starts to get tired. She catches a wave that carries her gently back to shore. Meanwhile, Matt and Daniel are still sitting on their surfboards in the ocean, waiting for the next set of waves to come in.

Daniel runs his fingers through his wet hair and looks inside his hand. "Shit! I think I'm starting to lose my hair. That sucks!"

Matt looks at his friend's receding hairline and runs his fingers through his own hair. When he looks in his hand, he sees only one strand of hair. "My hair is just turning gray."

"How's work?" Daniel asks.

Matt rolls his eyes. "Not exactly what I expected."

"You look beat, man. What happened to taking some time off and starting a family?"

"Tell me about it," Matt answers before taking a deep breath. "I should have stuck with the original plan. I don't think I ever totally got out of the doghouse because of that."

Daniel is amused. "What? You're still not off the hook with Kayla?"

"Nah, she still likes to remind me once in a while."

"I have to admit, Matt, I was surprised when you took that job. Whatever your motivation is, I'm sure it's a big deal for you."

"I thought it would be good for me if I followed in my dad's footsteps, but now I'm having second thoughts." Matt looks back at the beach, searching for his sweetheart. Kayla is sitting on a towel and putting on sunscreen. "She's right. Work always came first with me … If I had dedicated as much time and effort to my relationship with Kayla as I did with my career, we probably would have started a family by now."

"Hey, man, it's not too late," Daniel says.

"Yeah, I know … Family comes first. I don't want to lose her."

Matt is still looking at Kayla as she waves and blows a kiss to him.

Brentwood, Los Angeles

AT THE END OF A fun day surfing at the beach, Matt and Kayla are back at home and exhausted. Inside the garage, Matt takes one of the surfboards down from the SUV roof rack and leans it against the storage shelf. The weight from the surfboard pushes the old shelf to a breaking point, causing it to collapse. All of Cedric Schauberger's boxes fall on the floor in a messy pile.

"Damn it!" Matt exclaims with disbelief.

Kayla runs to the door and stares at the mess. She gives Matt the I-told-you-so expression. Matt holds his head, angry with himself for not listening to her earlier.

"I know," he admits. "I should have taken care of it sooner."

"I'm going to make dinner," Kayla says calmly. With that, Kayla leaves Matt by himself to clean the mess.

Great! he thinks to himself.

While he is cleaning up, Matt sees an open box on the floor with a bunch of photos next to it. Matt starts picking up the photos to put them back in the box without paying too much attention to them. Nevertheless, he becomes distracted by one picture that shows his father standing with a group of Tibetan monks. In the background of the picture, Matt recognizes a familiar painting of a Tibetan mandala. He takes the picture with him and walks in the house. He stops in front of the fireplace and sees the same mandala painting in the picture hanging over the fireplace. He lifts the framed mandala from the wall and starts to examine it with a closer eye. A sudden memory from his childhood comes back to him.

In the middle of the night, a nine-year-old Matthew is walking in his pajamas in the dark down the hallway of the house. He shows up half asleep in the study, where his dad is still working. In the dark, only using the desk lamp, Cedric is working at his desk and sees his son. He speaks to him in German.

"Did you have a nightmare again?" Matt nods sadly. "Come here, Son."

The young boy walks toward his dad and sits on his lap. The same mandala painting is on the desk. On top of it are notepads with mathematical equations, angle rulers, protractors, a drafting compass, and a calculator. Matt looks curiously at the mandala.

"What is this, Dad?" he asks.

"It's called a mandala … Since you're awake, maybe you can help me find its hidden secrets," Cedric says with a sense of adventure as he smiles at his son.

"What secret?" Matt asks with curiosity.

"A very old one. The man who gave this to me once said that this mandala holds encrypted information that could change everything we believe about the meaning of time … What do you see when you look at it?"

Matt looks carefully at the mandala. "I see a man sitting in the center … circles … squares. Hmmm." The young boy starts to tilt his head left and right. "When I do this, I feel like I'm looking though my kaleidoscope."

Cedric is intrigued. "A kaleidoscope?"

Matt runs to his room and comes back with his kaleidoscope. He gives it to his dad. Cedric looks through the tube, but it's too dark. "I can't see much."

"You have to look through it toward the light," Matt explains.

Cedric tries again toward the desk light, and Matt rotates the end of the tube for him. Cedric is looking through the optical lens and sees a myriad of bright colors and shapes moving in synchronicity. Suddenly, a flash of genius hits him. He examines the tube shape of the kaleidoscope for a moment from back to front and then turns to look at the mandala.

"What is it, Dad?" Matt asks.

"The diagram I'm looking for is encoded in 3-D," Cedric says as he points his finger to the golden-colored ring surrounding the Buddha in the center of the mandala. "He is an enlightened being, and the golden ring around him represents light." He then points his finger on the multiple circular ring layers and squares that give an illusion of depth of field. "Dimension." Finally, he uses his finger to make a circular rotation around the ring layers and tilts his head left and right. "Motion through space … How did I miss that? I'll be damned—the universe works in mysterious ways. Son, you're a genius!"

Matt is still in the living room, holding and tilting the mandala left and right. He hears a loose object moving behind the frame and takes a look to see what it is. As he flips over the mandala, a USB flash drive falls to the floor. Matt picks up the flash drive, runs upstairs to the study, and plugs it into the USB port of his computer.

On his monitor screen, the same Tibetan mandala is displayed and slowly breaks in to segments like a complex mathematical puzzle. In the center of the map, the golden color surrounding the Buddha turns to a vibrant, bright glow. As Matt watches, he remembers his dad's words. "Light," he whispers to himself.

The multiple ring layers detach from each other to give dimension. An animation shows the mandala turning in to a kind of 3-D map of a strange web universe. Various points located around the grid bend alternately to the center toward the Buddha figure. "Dimension."

Next, the rings separate into two groups and start to spin in opposite directions faster and faster. Everything on the screen is becoming brighter. "Motion through space and time."

Mathematical equations are now scrolling quickly, and blueprints of the time device are emerging on the screen. Staring at the monitor, Matt is shocked and amazed as he gazes at his father's lifetime of work.

"I'll be damned!" he mutters.

Chapter 6

Northridge, WTRD

IT IS MONDAY AT SEVEN o'clock in the morning, and Matt is already at the lab working. He hasn't felt this excited about his job in a long time. On his workstation is a new box with electronic component parts and everything he needs to make a new time-travel device. Matt reaches into his jacket pocket for the flash drive he found hidden in the mandala and plugs it into the computer USB port. Moments later, he opens the time device blueprint file directly from the flash drive.

"Here we go again!" he says to himself with an optimistic attitude.

For the next two weeks, Matt carefully welds the electronic components onto a new tiny circuit board and assembles the parts together. This time he only uses the USB flash drive database to program the device and to download software. Once the time device is complete, Matt secures it in the protective carbon fiber case. He then powers up the giant Tesla coils and gets them ready to test his new device for the ultimate trip.

With a new roll of yellow duct tape, Matt marks an *X* on the floor about twenty feet behind the Tesla coils, which are already spinning in full motion. Next, using the time device touch-screen interface, he enters the location coordinate data from where he stands and adds two minutes in the future in the time settings option. He then synchronizes his stopwatch with the time device for two minutes before he walks to the other side and distances himself fifteen feet from the Tesla coils.

"All right!" he announces to himself.

A moment later, Matt presses Enter on the flat-screen display. This time, it only takes a few seconds before a spark of light from the gateway connects with the metal ball on the time device he is holding.

"Woo! That's new!" Matt gasps, feeling a bit intimidated by the electrical discharge.

He quickly throws the device into the gateway and watches it vanish into thin air as the gateway collapses on itself like an implosion. The power source then shuts down, plunging the lab into total darkness. When the lights come back on, Matt is walking slowly toward the other side of the Tesla coils. A few seconds later, Matt looks at his stopwatch and begins to count down: "Three … two … one!"

Suddenly, out of nowhere, he hears a big bang and sees sparks shooting out from a single point. At that very moment, the time device falls to the floor a few inches from the yellow duct tape X mark. Amazingly, it did not appear to have any damage. The rookie scientist is astonished by the result.

"Outstanding!" he exclaims to himself. "Let's try again."

Matt spends the next three days doing further testing with the time device. One day, he even attaches his own GoPro camera to the protective case, hoping to catch on tape a glimpse of what the other side of the gateway looks like. Unfortunately, the camera comes back with only white noise recorded.

The floor in the lab now has dozens of yellow duct tape X marks, each one representing a successful reappearance at a different time and space.

Late one evening, Matt gets carried away and enters the location coordinates of the corridor leading to the lab into the time device. Even though he makes sure that no one is around and the doors are closed, the loud noise generated when the time device reappears causes some commotion with the security guards in the building. Although Matt had full authority to conduct the experiment and didn't have to explain anything to them, he decided not try that again.

Two weeks passed since Matt's first successful experiment with the new device. With multiple successes under his belt, Matt decides it time to take his experimentation to the next level. "Let's try something else," he says to himself with confidence.

He lays down a small wooden ramp in front of the Tesla coils and screws it tightly to the floor. Matt briefly leaves to lab and returns holding a small cage. He puts it down on the computer desk and takes out a little white mouse. "Come here, little one!"

Finding a lab mouse at the Waizer Corporation facility was not difficult, but he had to go shopping for the other thing he needed for his experiment. He went to a hobby store and bought a remote control monster truck. With everything he needs now ready to go, Matt mounts the time device onto the truck bed. Next, he opens the small door of the cab and puts the mouse inside.

"Sorry, Mousey. I couldn't find a DeLorean."

Matt doesn't like what he is about to do in the name of science, but his options to test the time machine on a living thing other than himself are limited.

"Have a safe trip," he says to the mouse.

With his final good-bye said, Matt powers up the Tesla coils. The process has become almost a routine. He enters the location coordinate data, including two minutes in the future on the time device touch screen and synchronizes his stopwatch. Next, he presses Enter and walks away, holding the remote control box in his hands. Using both joysticks, Matt drives the RC vehicle in position about twenty feet in front of the Tesla coils, which are spinning at full RPM. A few seconds pass, and a spark of light from the gateway connects with the metal ball on the time device. Matt pushes forward on the throttle control stick as the truck rapidly takes off and continues to accelerate toward the gateway. When the truck hits the wooden ramp, it jumps right into the gateway and vanishes.

Matt looks at his stopwatch and waits apprehensively for the final countdown. "Three … two … one …"

Suddenly, there's a big bang as sparks start shooting out from a single point. At that instant, the RC vehicle jumps out from the gateway. As the car races ahead at full speed, Matt realizes it doesn't seem to be slowing down.

"Oh no! Stop!" he yells as he takes the remote control box and pulls back the throttle stick.

The truck slows down and stops a few feet from the wall. Matt rushes toward it and quickly opens the cab door. The white mouse is alive and sniffing his way up to Matt's hand. At first glance, the mouse appears fine, but Matt still wants to bring it back to the animal lab for further analysis for any radiation exposure.

"Congratulations, you just made history!" Matt says to the mouse.

A few days later, Matt receives the test result from the animal lab and is relieved to discover that the mouse is perfectly healthy, without any trace of radiation.

Matt's next move is to make some changes to the time device by getting rid of the imposing soccer ball-shaped protective case. Using 3-D software, he designs a new, more compact protective case that can be mounted on his forearm. He saves the new blueprint design on a flash drive and takes it to a technician at the machine shop, where it will be built.

On his way back to the lab from the machine shop, Matt makes a call on his smartphone.

"Yes, I would like to speak to Mr. Waizer please … This is Matthew Schauberger."

"Mr. Waizer is on another line right now. Do you want to leave a message?" the CEO's personal assistant asks in response to Matt's request.

"Yes, please tell him to meet me at the lab in a hour," Matt says before hanging up.

About an hour later, Herbert arrives at the lab. The Tesla coils are already spinning in full motion. Using duct tape, Matt attaches the time device to a rolling office chair and then pushes it toward Herbert.

"Sir, can you please move a little to your left?" Matt instructs as he points at Herbert's feet.

The old man looks down and realizes that he is standing on an *X* created out of yellow duct tape.

"X marks the spot," Herbert jokes before moving ten feet away from it.

"Thank you! Now, watch this." Matt is fifteen feet from the gateway when he presses Enter on the touch screen. As soon as a spark of light from the gateway connects with the metal ball on the time device, he takes the office chair and throws it into the gateway. It vanishes, as expected, and the power flickers for a few seconds before coming back on at full strength. A minute and a half pass by without either of them saying a word. Suddenly, with a big bang, the office chair reappears ten feet from Herbert on the *X* mark. The old man flinches and stares at the chair for a moment.

"You did it! Congratulations, Matthew! You're truly your father's son."

"Thank you, sir!" Matt says with a smile.

Herbert walks closer to take a better look at the time device. "It didn't burn," he notes. "Incredible!"

"This one is different. I think the device is ready to be tested on a human subject," Matt announces.

Herbert is not convinced. "How can you be sure it's safe?"

Using his pocketknife, Matt cuts the duct tape and takes the device from the office chair. "I have tested it many times, and every attempt has been successful. Even a mouse specimen survived the trip … I would like to volunteer and test it myself."

"That is very brave of you, Matthew, but I don't think it's worth risking your life." Herbert starts to walk toward the exit door.

"Please, sir, this is extremely important to me, especially if this can help me find out what happened to my dad. I wouldn't volunteer if I had any doubts about its safety."

Herbert stops. After a brief pause, he says, "Listen, let me think about it, and I'll get back to you."

With that, he leaves the lab, leaving Matt with hope that the old man will make the right decision.

Chapter 7

Brentwood, Los Angeles

KAYLA AND MATT ARE AT home having dinner. In the background, the news channel is playing on the TV in the living room. Presidential Candidate Andrew Cooper is making a speech. "I say we bring all our troops home. Our dependency on fossil fuel has got to come to an end. We will secure our economy and our national security by investing in our future right here at home in alternative clean energy sources."

The anchorman takes over and talks about the election. "The race is still head-to-head, and both candidates have very different opinions about—"

"Cooper gets my vote on this one," Kayla says.

"Don't say that to my boss," Matt jokes.

He has been looking pale lately, and Kayla is starting to worry about him. "You look tired."

Matt smiles at her. "I'm fine … I finally had a breakthrough at work."

"Let me guess—you can't talk about it."

Matt takes a deep breath and holds his head. "Come on, babe, please don't do that to me," he pleads.

"All right, but you've been working too much. All work and no play makes Matt a dull boy."

"What?" Matt is taken aback by the comment.

"Let's do something fun. You need a break." Kayla gets closer and sits on Matt's lap.

"What do you have in mind?"

Kayla doesn't have to think about it long. "Let's have a little getaway next weekend—just you and me. How about Napa Valley?"

Matt likes the idea. "You know what? Let's do it."

"Really?" Kayla asks, not expecting Matt to go along with her idea so easily.

"Yeah, you're right. We both deserve a break. Besides, I could certainly use a drink or two."

Kayla hugs him, and they kiss.

"Me too!" she says.

Matt is really looking forward to their trip together, but his mind is still preoccupied with another kind of trip.

Northridge, WTRD

TWO DAYS AFTER THE CONVERSATION the couple had about taking a trip, Matt is back in the lab at Waizer Corp. He is placing the time device in the new streamline carbon fiber protective case, and it fits like a glove.

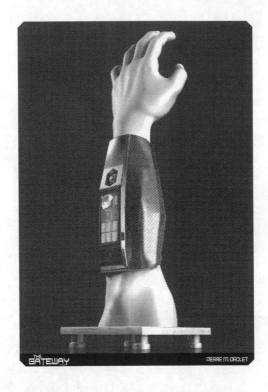

Earlier in the day, he'd received a phone call from the technician at the machine shop telling him his special order was ready for pick up. Now that he's back at the lab, Matt rolls up the left sleeve of his shirt and straps the time device around his forearm. "Not bad," he says to himself.

Matt's attention is distracted by the sounds from the mechanism of the lab door opening. He rolls back down his sleeve over the time device as Herbert and a special guest walk into the lab.

"Good afternoon, Matthew," Herbert says. "Look

who I brought with me—the next president of the United States."

Matt is surprised and gradually walks toward the men. Karl Waizer gives him a handshake.

"Nice to see you, sir," Matt says as he greets Waizer's son.

"Long time no see, Matt. First, I want to thank you for your service to our country and, secondly, for your contribution to the recent scientific breakthrough at Waizer Corporation."

"Thank you, sir."

"And, by the way, please call me Karl. *Sir* is for my father."

Herbert comes closer to Matt and calmly grabs his shoulder. "I have given some thought to your proposal. Are you sure you want to do this?" he asks.

Matt doesn't have any second thoughts. With determination, he replies, "Yes, sir."

"Very well then. I have only one request before you proceed."

"What is it?" Matt asks.

"The election is in three days. To make this epic trip something special between us, I would like you to travel to the future, one day after the election, and find out if my son will win the presidency," Herbert explains.

Matt thinks about it for a second, and the proposition

seems fair at first sight. "All right, I'll do it. I'll be back with the answer."

"Very well then," Herbert says before going on with the directives. "Four days from now, I will be here in the lab to give you the election results. Good luck!"

Matt nods and starts to power up the Tesla coils before walking over to the yellow duct tape X on the floor. He pulls up his sleeve and begins to enter the location coordinates data on the touch-screen display of the time device, including four days added in the future. He then moves twenty-five feet from the Tesla coils, which are already spinning in full motion. He looks back at Herbert and Karl who are both standing at a safe distance behind him. Matt gives the *okay* signal.

"Here we go!" he announces.

When he hits the Enter key on the touch screen of the time device, it only takes a second before a spark of light from the gateway connects with the metal ball on the time device. He takes a deep breath before he starts to run as fast as he can toward the gateway and jumps into it before vanishing out of sight.

Inside the Gateway

INITIALLY, THE LAB FADES TO a radiant emptiness. Then, multiple beams of light start to move slowly, creating geometric patterns. Matt is not sure if he's trapped or frozen in time, but the feeling doesn't last long.

Suddenly, the space around him begins to morph to some kind of a funnel cloud filled with rays of light. As the time traveler is pulled into it, everything is moving faster and faster on a massive scale. A blinding light forms, and Matt is rushed right through it.

Four Days in the Future

IN THE LAB, MATT REAPPEARS from sparks of light out of nowhere as he falls a foot from the yellow X taped on the floor. He feels a little disoriented and nauseous for a few seconds.

A familiar voice snaps him out of it. "Are you all right?"

Matt is on his knees and looks up at Herbert. "Yeah, I think so."

"You did it, Matthew!" Herbert announces. "Welcome to the future."

Matt stands up and looks around. "Where's Karl?" he asks.

Herbert is holding a newspaper and gives it to Matt. On the first page, Andrew Cooper is celebrating his victory as the new president of the United States. Matt gives the newspaper back to the old man. "I'm sorry, sir. I hate to be the messenger of bad news. I know you will be very disappointed."

Herbert walks to the main control area and powers

up the Tesla coils. "It's okay, Matthew. It's not the end of the world. You did good … Have a safe trip."

"Yeah, thank you, sir."

Once again, Matt jumps back into the gateway and vanishes between the Tesla coils.

Four Days Earlier, Present Day

BACK IN THE LAB, MATT reappears from sparks of light that seem to come out of nowhere as he jumps out and lands on the concrete floor. Herbert and Karl are standing a few feet in front of him. Matt is disoriented and nauseous again. He looks down at his feet and sees the yellow *X* marked on the floor.

"Is everything all right, Matthew?" Herbert asks.

"Yes … yes, I think so."

"Do you have the answer to my question?"

Matt is holding his head, as he is still disoriented and experiencing a momentary loss of focus.

Karl is anxious to know the answer to his dad's question. "Am I going to be the next president of the United States?"

There is much trepidation as Matt looks at both of them. "I'm sorry I have to bring you bad news. It's not going to happen … Cooper wins."

Herbert and Karl look at each other in disbelief.

"I'm very sorry," Matt says sincerely as Herbert grabs his shoulder.

"It's okay, Matthew. It's not the end of the world. You did good … I'm just glad you came back safely."

"Thank you, sir. Talk about déjà vu. In the future, you just said the same thing to me a few minutes ago."

Karl looks at his watch and seems agitated. "Well, I have to go now … I still have a campaign to run. Matt, thank you. It was nice seeing you again."

"Good-bye, sir," Matt says. "It was good to see you too."

Herbert looks at his son walking away before looking back at Matt with his usual smirk on his face. "I'll talk to you later."

With that, Herbert and Karl exit the lab.

Chapter 8

MATT HAS EVERY REASON TO be proud of himself after accomplishing this astonishing milestone. He still hasn't quite figured out how he will use the time machine to search for answers about what happened to his father, but he feels one step closer. An initial thought was to go back in time about a year and a half when Cedric was still alive and warn him not to jump into the gateway. But the time traveler is aware of the paradox effect where he can create two of himself on the same timeline. This scenario could be catastrophic. For this reason, Matt's not thrilled about the idea.

By the end of the day, a lot of pressure is off of Matt's shoulders, and his mind-set, for once, is not about work. To celebrate the special occasion, Matt decides to take both his sweetheart and his best friend to a casual gathering at a restaurant-bar in Santa Monica. The Lakers game is being shown on a flat-screen TV, but Matt, Kayla, and Daniel aren't paying any attention to the game. They're enjoying each other's company and having a good time, as they welcome the second round of beer pitcher brought to the table by the waitress.

Matt raises his glass and says, "I'd like to make a toast! To the woman I love and to friendship … I love you guys! Salut!"

Kayla and Daniel raise their glass as they yell out in unison. "Cheers!"

"Wow, you're in a really good mood," Kayla says to Matt.

Daniel seems to never miss an occasion to be sarcastic with his buddy. "This doesn't sound like you, Matty boy. You're not dying are you?"

"No … A lot of pressure lifted off my shoulders recently," Matt answers with a smile.

"That secret job of yours has been draining the life out of you," Kayla says. "I don't know what happened, but I'm glad to have you back."

After a few rounds of beer, Matt soon loosens up. "The only thing I can tell you guys is … my dad was a goddamned genius." At this point, Matt is a bit intoxicated and uninhibited from the alcohol.

Those last words pique Kayla's curiosity, and she decides to act on it. "All right, man of mystery … You know we can find a lot of information on the Internet." Kayla takes out her iPad from her purse and starts a Google search for Matt's father.

"What are you doing?" Matt asks.

She starts typing *Cedric Schauberger* on the Google home page. "I'm sure we can find something about your dad ... Let's see what comes up."

The first thing Kayla notices is a few conspiracy theory websites that have popped up. Kayla clicks the link to one of them, while Daniel looks over her shoulder.

"Wow! Conspiracy theory?!" Daniel looks at Matt and makes a spooky face. "What was your dad working on again?"

Matt remains silent but is a bit annoyed at the unsolicited inquiry about his father.

"Here we go!" Kayla starts to read the website. "*Cedric Schauberger, scientist. Mostly known for his research on quantum mechanics and electromagnetic pulse technology.* That's interesting," Kayla says in a cocky way before continuing. "Does this have anything to do with what you're working on?"

As she unknowingly gets closer to the truth, Matt starts to feel uneasy. "All right," he says. "You had your fun."

"Are you kidding me?! I'm just getting started. Where were we ... ah!" Kayla starts to read the webpage again. "*Cedric Schauberger was born in the United States, and there is speculation that he is the legitimate son of a German scientist named Viktor Schauberger. At the end of the war, in 1945, Viktor Schauberger and about 150 other Nazi scientists surrendered to US troops ... and they were all integrated into the American scientific community under the code name 'Operation Paperclip.'"*

This last paragraph really captures Matt's attention. "What? Let me see that. This has to be a mistake," he exclaims.

Daniel is a bit confused with this clandestine information. "You never told me your grandfather was a Nazi."

Matt starts to wonder if this information about Viktor Schauberger has anything to do with what Herbert Waizer once told him: *"Your family history has been hidden from you for your own protection."* If this were all true, it would imply his father might have also lied about his ancestry. But how could this be true? Matt desperately thought to himself. His first reaction is denial, and he rejects the information immediately.

"C'mon, man! It's a conspiracy theory website," Matt points out. "Besides, my dad never met his biological parents. He was just an infant when a German family adopted him in Arizona."

"Maybe your dad's adoptive father was the Nazi scientist," Daniel suggests.

"I doubt that. I never met him because he died before I was born. I do know for a fact his name was not Viktor," Matt replies.

Looking for more information, curiosity turns to a guilty pleasure for Kayla. She jokingly remarks, "I still want to know more about this alternative story ... Now this is getting very interesting. I want to know more about your *conspiracy* grandfather."

Matt doesn't find any of this amusing in the least bit. "Seriously, babe, that's enough."

Kayla types the name *Viktor Schauberger* into Google and opens one of the websites. "Zip it!" she snaps at Matt before beginning to read again. *"Viktor Schauberger is known as the father of the Haunebu Project."*

"Never heard of it," Daniel says as he looks at his friend, expecting an answer.

"Neither have I," Matt responds.

As much as Matt wants Kayla to stop reading, he is curious to hear more.

She continues on. *"He dedicated his life to developing electromagnetic pulse engine technology. Throughout World War II, he was also deeply involved with an underground Nazi organization called Vril Society."*

"Dude! That's a weird coincidence! Your father and this guy did the same kind of work," Daniel cries out.

"No shit," Matt says in disbelief.

Kayla scrolls down and finds a black-and-white photograph dated November 9, 1944, from Nazi

Germany. It shows two Nazi officers and three scientists wearing white lab coats standing side by side. "Let's see," Kayla says, "which one is your grandfather in this photo?"

"Stop calling that Nazi my grandfather!" Matt snaps at her, a bit irritated.

"Sorry!" she says with a smug look on her face.

Daniel is amused by his friend's reaction, as both come closer to Kayla for a better look. Matt finds *Viktor Schauberger* written under the picture and points at one of the scientists. "That's him … the man with the beard."

Kayla is distracted by the Nazi officers on the right side of the picture, but after taking a closer look, she gets chills down her back. "Oh my God! Look at this guy … He looks just like you."

"Holy shit, you're right." Daniel can't believe what he sees. He starts to laugh and says, "Wait a minute here! Are you guys pranking me? That's photoshopped, right?"

Matt shakes his head no. He looks at the two other scientists in the picture, and one of them catches his attention. In disbelief, he recognizes his father. Matt's eyes light up as he whispers to himself, "He's alive!"

Kayla and Daniel both give him a puzzled look. Matt is pointing at one of the scientists. "That's my dad!"

She stares at the photo in disbelief and recognizes him too. "Okay, this is not funny anymore. What's going on here? Now you're starting to freak me out."

On the live TV, the Lakers game is interrupted for a special news report. All of the patrons in the restaurant turn their attention to the screen. The anchorman addresses the nation. "Just a few minutes ago, Presidential Candidate Andrew Cooper was shot. He was pronounced dead at the scene at 10:35 p.m. Eastern time."

As the news anchor speaks, video footage of the assassination is being played. It shows Cooper walking on a stage and his head being blown off by a sniper shot. He falls to the floor and doesn't move. All of the Secret Service people are running around in panic.

"Senator Waizer has just learned about the news," the anchorman says.

Another segment of video footage shows Karl Waizer being interview. "I just heard about the horrible news. I would like to convey my sincere condolences to the Cooper family, and my prayers are with them." Karl becomes visibly emotional as he speaks. "I'm sorry. I cannot talk right now. May God rest his soul in peace."

Matt cannot believe what just happened. Knowing what he knows, he sees the tragedy differently than everyone else around him. "This is a nightmare!"

"Yeah, I can't believe this is happening," Kayla says, totally distracted by the horrible news.

"You don't understand. He was not supposed to die. He was going to be the next president," Matt blurts out.

Daniel is perplexed as to why his friend seems to be taking the tragedy so personally. "What in the world are you talking about? Nobody knows that for sure."

"Yes, I do! This is all my fault. We have to get out of here."

"What!?" Kayla questions, clearly confused.

Matt quickly stands up and throws four twenty-dollar bills on the table. "Now!" he demands, firmly grabbing Kayla's hand and briskly walking out the restaurant. Daniel follows close behind.

The three friends climb into Matt's SUV, which is parked on the street. As Matt starts the engine, he looks around to be sure no one has followed them. Daniel doesn't know what is going on, but he has a bad feeling his friend might be in deep trouble.

"What's going on?" Daniel asks, breaking the silence. "Are we being followed?"

"I don't know," Matt admits.

Matt steps on the gas and drives east toward the 405 freeway.

After all the commotion at the restaurant, Kayla is more determined than ever to find out what Matt is hiding from her. "Okay, Matthew, now you're scaring me. If you know something we don't, now would be a good time to talk."

"I have a strong suspicion that Andrew Cooper's assassination was set up by Herbert and Karl Waizer," Matt reveals.

Kayla had not expected to hear this. "That is some serious accusation. Do you have any proof of that?" she asks.

"Yes … Well, no! I'm the one who gave them the information. So stupid! Now Cooper is dead because of me."

Daniel is confused. "You're not making any sense, Matt. How exactly are you involved with Cooper's death?"

Kayla already knows the answer, but she wants to hear it from Matt. "Does this have anything to do with your job?" she questions.

Matt takes a deep breath before answering. "Yeah …
I've been using my dad's work to perfect a device that
would allow me to move between different point in time
as well as space."

Kayla and Daniel both stare at Matt with a
puzzled look.

"*A time machine!*" Matt exclaims.

Daniel had heard what his friend had just said, but
he is not quite sure what to think about this sudden
confession. "Oh! Okay … why didn't you just say that
to begin with?" Daniel jokingly replies.

"I'm not kidding. I used it to travel to the future
to find out who would win the presidential election.
I came back and gave the answer to the Waizers
this morning." Matt looks at them with an honest,
straight face.

"I know that face … You're telling the truth, aren't
you?" Kayla asks.

Matt nods. He has a shameful look on his face. "The
purpose of that trip was supposed to just test the effect
on a human, but instead, Waizer used me for his son's
political agenda."

Kayla is furious. "Matthew! What the hell were you
thinking?"

"Obviously, I wasn't. My only objective was to use
the time machine to find my dad. He didn't die in a
plane crash, and now I know where he is."

Kayla starts to connect the dots. "You mean the man in the picture could really be your dad?"

Matt nods.

Daniel looks at his friend with disbelieve. "That's messed up, man."

For each answer Matt gives away, Kayla has ten more questions. "But how did he end up in Nazi Germany?" she asks.

"I don't know," Matt answers. "But right now I'm responsible for what happened to Cooper, and I have to do something about it."

"God! I'm so mad at you right now. I thought you knew better than that!" Kayla says. She is clearly having a hard time controlling her emotions.

"Look, I know I screwed up big time," Matt confesses. "I created this mess, and I'm going to fix it."

Kayla has a bad feeling about what exactly Matt has in mind. "How? Don't you think it's a little too late?"

"Not if you have a time machine," Matt says with confidence.

After driving for thirty five minutes, the three friends arrive at a destination in Northridge, and Matt stops the SUV a few blocks from the Waizer Corporation building. When she realizes where they are, Kayla firmly grabs on to Matt's arm. "Oh no! Absolutely not! This is totally out of the question!"

Daniel doesn't like the idea either. "I'm with Kayla on this one. I don't think you should use that thing again."

"All right, then I'm just going to destroy it." Matt pulls a USB flash drive out of his jacket pocket and gives it to Kayla. "Hang on to this as if your life depends on it. I'm glad I never downloaded its contents on the network."

"What is this?" Kayla asks.

Matt doesn't answer the question and gets out of the SUV. He looks back at her and smiles before he starts to walk toward the building. Daniel and Kayla rush after him.

"Hey! Where do you think you're going?!" Kayla asks in a scared tone. She is on the verge of crying.

Daniel stops his friend in his path. "Matt, wait!"

"Go back to the car," Matt says with an authoritarian tone.

Daniel steps in front of Matt and yells out. "Listen to me! We should not be here. It's not safe at all. You're making it too easy for Waizer by walking straight into the lion's mouth."

"I gave Waizer a fully operational time machine, and he's obviously up to no good," Matt responds. "This is probably the last chance I have to get my hands on the time device and destroy it."

The military brotherhood bond between the two friends is strong, and Daniel decides to go along with Matt's plan. "I'm going with you then," he finally says.

Matt values Daniel's loyalty but knows this is a one-man mission. He gently grabs his friend's shoulder. "No, you stay here with Kayla. You will not pass the security checkpoint, and I don't want to draw any attention to myself. If I'm not back in twenty minutes, I want you to take her to a safe place. Understood?"

Daniel doesn't like the idea but understands Matt's point of view. "Yeah."

Kayla feels like she is in a nightmare and can't wake up. "What?" she exclaims with disbelief.

"I'm sorry, baby," Matt says. "Because of what I did, I've put all of our lives in danger. I don't want to take any chances. If something happens to me, that means you're next on the list. I won't let that happen."

"But, you don't really think—" She can't finish her sentence as she envisions the worst-case scenario of losing him.

Matt moves away from them. "If anyone asks you, we never had this conversation … I'll be back in twenty minutes."

As Matt starts to run toward the industrial facility, Kayla goes after him. "Matthew, wait!" she calls out.

"I'm sorry, babe," Matt yells back without stopping. "I should have listened to you! I love you!"

Kayla stops in her path and yells at the top of her lungs. "Matt!"

He turns back to look at her one last time and then keeps running.

Northridge, WTRD

WHEN MATT ARRIVES AT THE gated main entrance, he scans and shows his ID card to the security guard. "Hey, Ben."

"Hey, Matt, working late tonight?"

"Yeah."

The security guard has gotten used to seeing Matt come in and out of the facility for the past six months. He salutes Matt and lets him in. As Matt walks through the security gate, he's relieved that his ID card still works. He rushes toward the lab.

A few minutes later, Matt arrives at the lab in front of the steel door. Nervously, he swipes his ID card and enters a security code. Multiple green lasers scan his body as he impatiently waits for the door to open. "Come on!" he mutters.

Multiple click sounds from the lock mechanism can be heard as it opens. As soon as the doors open, Matt hears the unexpected but familiar loud electromagnetic stormy noise of the Tesla coils spinning at full RPM.

"Shit!" he exclaims as he begins to run for the lab, hoping that no one would use the time machine that is in motion. The door automatically closes behind him, and he sees Herbert Waizer standing in the dark about twenty feet from the Tesla coils. He is holding the time device and staring at the gateway.

The old man takes a deep breath and yells at him. "Matthew, I have been waiting for you."

He walks toward Herbert. "You set me up! Why did you do that?"

"Don't take it personally. It was just the right thing to do. I told you before; my son will be a better president," Herbert says calmly.

"You have no right to change the natural course of events. By killing Cooper, you destroyed his fate to become the true president ... You murderer!"

Herbert gives Matt his usual smirk. "Natural course of events? The last time I heard those words it was your father speaking. I had high expectations for you, and you certainly delivered. If anyone was going to find Cedric's missing files, I figured it would be his own son."

Matt is furious. "What did you do to him?" he demands.

"I didn't kill your father. I'm not responsible for what happened to him. He did it to himself!"

Matt reacts discreetly when he realizes they are not alone—a tactical team surrounds the dark room. Matt tries to stay calm.

"I didn't say anything about killing him. You have a lot of blood on your hands, old man," Matt angrily remarks.

Herbert takes a look around the lab at the tactical team, closes his eyes, and gives a nod. "Take him out!"

At the same time, Matt jumps on Herbert and firmly grabs him. Four men armed with handguns rush out from their hiding places. The team leader yells at Matt. "Freeze! Let him go! Let him go now!"

Matt reaches for the time device in Herbert's hands and manages to turn it on, but the old man has a tight grip on it and doesn't let go.

"How dare you! Let me go!" Herbert demands. He tries to fight, but Matt has a solid grip on him.

"Let him go now!" the team leader orders one more time.

Matt knows too well that if he lets go, he is as good as dead. "Tell them to drop their weapons!" Matt yells out as he tries to gain some time.

"You are in no position to make any demands!" Herbert argues in a feisty tone.

"All right, then you're coming with me … Let's see how far you can bounce!"

Matt presses the Enter key on the time device touch screen as he starts to run toward the gateway, lifting and pushing Herbert with him.

"Noooo!" Herbert is screaming at the top of his lungs as the get closer and closer to the gateway. "Noooo! You're crazy!" In desperation, Herbert gives an order to the tactical team. "Shut down the power! Shut it down!"

Right before they hit the gateway, Matt rips the time

device from Herbert's hands and lets him go. He then jumps into the gateway and vanishes. The results are different for his captive. When Herbert hits the gateway, his body gets burned and then bounces violently into the air before landing lifeless on the floor.

The gateway collapses on itself like an implosion and then expands violently, releasing devastating lightning bolts. One of them bursts through the ceiling and reaches the sky.

Two blocks away from the Waizer Corporation, Kayla and Daniel are standing in the street. They are terrified and expect that the worst has just happened as they witness the explosive scene. Daniel glances around the area and sees nobody. He then looks at Kayla and knows what he has to do.

"Come on. We gotta go."

Chapter 9

Somewhere in Time

THE GATEWAY OPENS WITH A big bang, and Matt is ejected out from it. He takes a hard fall and drops the time device on a dusty floor. He attempts to stand up but is still weak from the force of the gateway and falls back down.

As he nervously looks around, it appears that he is alone and still in the lab. However, the place looks quite different from when he last saw it before jumping through the gateway. The two giant Tesla coils once stood a few feet behind him, but now all the equipments and electronics were gone. The lab looks more like an empty warehouse that has been abandoned for many years. In fact, the lab is so worn down that a section of the ceiling is missing, allowing the sunlight to shine through the big gap. Matt feels a bit dizzy and disoriented as he stands up again.

Unbeknownst to Matt, mounted on the wall is a

motion-activated security camera, which has just been activated. In front of the camera is an infrared light, which turns on.

As Matt is slowly gaining back his strength, he starts to wonder what happened to the lab and what year is he in. "Okay … at least I'm alive," Matt says to himself. He picks up the scratched time device still on the floor. The screen display cover is cracked and is showing a blue screen with error codes. "Great, just what I need!"

He turns off the time device and straps it around his forearm. While walking toward the exit, he conceals the time device under his leather jacket sleeve. The massive vault door is locked, requiring Matt to find another way out. Luckily, he spots a broken vent shaft up on the wall. By using one of the vertical pipes on the wall, he starts to climb his way up. When he reaches about fifteen feet above the ground, Matt comes across a security camera he had never seen before in the old lab.

That's new, he thinks to himself.

He knows what this security camera had just recorded and realizes the potential danger looming ahead. He is now more determined than ever to get out of there, especially since his last encounter with Herbert in the lab almost cost him his life. Matt rips the security camera from the wall and throws it on the floor.

Thousands of Miles Away in an Underground Military Base

DOZENS OF MILITARY PERSONNEL ARE working in a command control room. Footage from a security camera recording video pops up on a computer screen, followed by the sound of an alarm. A military officer sitting at the workstation desk diverts his attention to the video. He views the footage, which shows heavy static distortion followed by Matt falling to the floor of the lab.

"Where did you come from?" the military officer asks, looking at the screen. He immediately picks up the phone and makes a call. "Give me the president."

Washington, DC, White House

TWELVE HIGH-RANKING MILITARY OFFICIALS ARE in the Oval Office meeting with the president, who is sitting behind his desk. A military officer enters the office and heads directly toward the president. The military officer whispers something in his ear and leaves. The news gets his immediate attention.

"Gentlemen, please excuse me. I have to adjourn this meeting," the president says.

Everybody exits the Oval Office as the president picks up the phone. "This is the president." The man is an older Karl Waizer.

"Mr. President, I just received a video surveillance transmission of unusual activity from Ground X," the military officer says from the command control room.

Karl pauses for a second. "Send it to me."

"Yes, Mr. President."

Karl looks at his computer screen monitor and watches the video of Matt's arrival. His beady eyes open wide when he spots the time device.

"I got you, you son of a bitch!" Karl says under his breath. He quickly turns his attention to the military officer waiting on the phone and gives his orders. "Call the Air Force! I want two Vrils ready for immediate departure for a retrieval mission. Location: Ground X, Northridge, California. Target identified as Matthew Schauberger."

"But … sir, Northridge is under the control of the Resistance," the military officer protests. "We have an—"

Karl interrupts before he can finish his sentence. "You have my orders. Send a unit now!"

"Yes, Mr. President. Right away."

Karl hangs up the phone and anxiously views the security camera footage again.

Northridge, WTRD

BACK AT THE FACILITY, MATT is crawling into the dark vent shaft and finally reaches the other end to a potential exit. He has to give the vent cover a hard push before it falls and opens the narrow exit. He then pulls himself out before jumping on the floor of a deserted corridor. From there, Matt finds his way out of the building, still without encountering any sign of life. The sun is setting fast as he runs out of the Waizer Corporation facility. When he reaches the street, he notices it is eerily quiet. The power is out, and the whole industrial park looks like a disaster area.

"What in the hell happened here?" he says to himself.

Matt walks down the deserted street a few blocks before hearing the sound of jet engines. He sees three fighter jets fly by, although he cannot identify them clearly. As he continues to walk, another engine noise can be heard down the street. He sees a military vehicle turning toward him.

Matt begins to run. "Hey! Wait!" he yells after them.

The armored truck is moving in his direction as he is walking toward them. Behind the first Humvee are four other military vehicles, and two of them are armored truck troopers. On top of the Humvee, the turret gunner points his .50 caliber machine gun directly at Matt.

"What happened here?" Matt asks the gunner while slowly raising his hands up in the air.

The Humvee stops at a safe distance from him. "Don't move! Put your hands up!" the gunner orders.

"What's going on here?" Matt has a lot of questions that will have to wait. He has no choice but to comply with the order to raise his hands higher over his head.

"Turn around and get down on your knees!" a voice yells from the Humvee.

Suddenly, thirty armed soldiers jump out from both armored trucks. Three of them aim their assault rifles at Matt while they walked toward him.

"You are trespassing in a restricted military area," one of the soldiers says. "Are there others here with you?"

Matt is distracted by the unusual gear and assault rifles on the soldiers but still answers the question. "No. I'm alone"

The head soldier gives his order to the platoon. "Check the perimeter."

At the same time, a second soldier takes out a device no larger than a small torchlight and places it in front of Matt's eyes. A blue laser scans his eyes, but out of reflex he blinks.

"Keep your eyes open," the soldier directs. After three trials, the device emits the same beeping sound indicating a negative ID. "He's not in the system."

The soldier starts to search inside Matt's jacket and finds his wallet. Matt has his back to the convoy and hears a door slam closed from the Humvee.

Staff Sergeant Palmer, a well-built African American male in his late twenties, walks up to him. "Stand up and turn around!" Palmer orders with an authoritarian tone.

Matt turns around as the staff sergeant begins walking toward him. On his left side, a soldier begins to scan Matt's ID with an eyeglasses, and the information is transmitted to the command center. Staff Sergeant Palmer stops a few inches away from Matt and stands face-to-face with him. "Your name?" he questions.

"Matthew Schauberger."

"Are you civilian or military?"

Matt thinks it's an odd question to ask but looks at him straight in the eyes and answers. "I'm a Marine vet."

"What are you doing here?" Palmer asks.

Matt has to think about this question for a second before responding. "I'm just passing through."

"That's not a good answer! I'll repeat only one more time! What are you doing here?"

Palmer is interrupted by the soldier who had scanned Matt's ID. "Staff Sergeant!"

The soldier whispers something in Palmer's ear and then hands him Matt's ID. They both look perplexed. Palmer turns his attention back to Matt.

"Where did you get this ID?"

Matt looks at his driver's license and has only one answer for them. "The DMV."

Both men stare at him for a second, not at all amused as Matt would expect.

"You're under arrest for trespassing. Bring him in," Palmer says as he turns around and walks back to the Humvee. He then gives the order to his troop. "Reassemble! We're heading back to base."

As a soldier grabs on to Matt's arm, a crackling noise and an eerie, high-pitched sound can be heard approaching. All the soldiers stop dead in their tracks and hold their rifles tightly. A frightening feeling begins to grow among the soldiers as they all look up in the sky.

"Oh, shit!" the soldier holding on to Matt exclaims before suddenly letting him go. He points up to the sky. "Over there!"

Matt's mouth drops open at the sight of two flying saucers hovering over a building. He estimates they must be fifty feet in diameter. "Noooo way!" He can't believe his eyes.

"Take cover!" Palmer yells out loud.

A night-vision camera mounted under the flying saucer records the scene from above. The soldiers on the street are frantically running away to find cover. The camera scans the area and stops on Matt.

Inside the flying saucer, the pilot reports his newly obtained information through a secure communication channel. "Target identified. The Resistance found him first. Stand by. Ready to engage."

White House, Oval Office

KARL IS SITTING AT HIS desk watching the same footage on his computer screen of Matt wearing civilian clothing, making him stands out from the soldiers. He gives his orders to the pilot over the phone. "I want him alive, but get rid of the others."

"Roger that, Fox One!" the pilot replies.

Karl hangs up the phone and turns off his computer monitor.

Northridge

BACK IN THE STREET OF the industrial park, a guided missile is fired from one of the saucer-shaped aircraft. It hits and destroys the first Humvee. Matt is thrown to the ground from the blast. Moments later, two other guided missiles from the second saucer hit the two armored truck troopers, destroying both of them. The soldiers return fire with their rifles. One of the soldiers in charge of the communication calls for back up.

"Mayday! Mayday! We're under attack! Need air support now!"

Matt is still on the ground, trying to come back to his senses. He feels himself lift up as Palmer grabs his leather jacket.

"C'mon! Get up!" Palmer orders.

There are loud noises and explosions everywhere. The saucers fire on surrounding building walls where the soldiers are taking refuge. One of the two remaining Humvees takes off as the gunner on top blasts at the saucers, but unfortunately, it's not enough to bring down the aircraft. One of the saucers shoots back with a violent death ray. The armored truck is thrown into the air and smashes against a building wall. On impact, the gunner is ejected from the Humvee.

Palmer spots the last Humvee covered in debris. "Let's go!" he yells out.

Matt and Palmer run to the armored truck, clear the wreckage away from the door, and then quickly jump inside. The staff sergeant starts the engine and drives the Humvee through the wreckage. One of the saucers changes course and goes after them. Palmer looks in his rearview mirror and sees the saucer tailing behind him.

"We've got company!" he exclaims. "Get down!"

A death ray beam aimed in their direction misses the target, but the shockwave generated by the explosion on the ground almost flips over the Humvee. Palmer makes a sharp turn and drives directly through the glass window of a building, crushes everything in its path, and comes out the other side.

"Hang on!" Palmer says before they land in an alleyway.

Matt checks around for any sign of the flying saucer. "There!" he points out. "Four o'clock!"

The staff sergeant slams on the accelerator as he drives the armored truck in to the alleyway, hoping the flying saucer hadn't spotted them.

"We can't stay in the open. We have to find a place to hide," Palmer says apprehensively.

He makes a sharp left turn onto the main street and keeps going for a few blocks. The option for cover in the area is limited. Matt sees an abandoned Costco warehouse down the street, which seems to be their best option if they can stay off the radar detection. "Over there!"

The saucer is out of sight, and Palmer takes the opportunity to quickly drive the Humvee across the street to the Costco parking lot. He drives the armored truck behind the warehouse and into the delivery area, breaking through one of the garage doors. Boxes, racks, and inventory of all kinds are flying around over the Humvee's hood until Palmer hits the brakes. The Humvee stops in the dark Costco warehouse, leaving behind a messy trail of wreckage.

Matt and Palmer both stay quiet until the staff sergeant speaks up. "We'll wait till things quiet down a bit. You mind?"

Matt just looks at him as he is catching his breath,

not sure if Palmer is being serious, sarcastic, or both. Unfortunately, they are not out of danger. Suddenly, the beam of a death ray passes straight through the warehouse roof and blows up everything in its path. The blast creates a devastating inferno.

"Damn it!" Matt ducks and covers his ears. Palmer steps on the gas, steering the armored truck through the rubble as he desperately looks for an exit. The visibility is poor, and his options are becoming limited as the Humvee charges toward the far wall. The room for error is small; there is just enough space between two structural steel H beams for the Humvee to pass through.

"Hang on to something!" Palmer yells.

The armored truck crashes through the brick wall and ends up in the parking lot. Both side mirrors are gone, as is the gun turret. One of the saucers flies over the Humvee at low altitude and turns around for a face-off. The staff sergeant hits the brakes, and the military vehicle stops. The men are now staring at the menacing saucer.

"Get back! Get back!" Matt cries out, his voice filled with anxiety.

The Humvee engine stalls, and Palmer is desperately trying to start it. "C'mon!" he begs.

Just when both men think it is over for them, a friendly, unusual-looking fighter jet fires one electromagnetic pulse (EMP) missile at the saucer. Upon impact, the explosion disturbs the force field around the saucer's hull. A second EMP missile strikes again and successfully shuts it down completely. Another unusual-looking fighter jet joins the fight and keeps shooting with its 20mm machine gun at the saucer head.

"Yeah! Here comes the cavalry!" Palmer says with excitement as he tries to start the engine.

The saucer falls and crashes into the cars in an open parking lot. The parked cars take most of the impact, leaving the saucer with superficial damage to the hull. "What the hell was that?" Matt asks.

Palmer ignores him as the engine finally starts. He adjusts his earpiece by pressing a button clipped on his tactical vest. "Piece of shit!" he yells in frustration. "Never works when you need it." The staff sergeant throws the earpiece in the backseat and drives back to the main street. When the chaos has finally ended, Matt breathes a sigh of relief and gives thanks that he's alive.

"I'm taking you to the base," Palmer says.

Matt is having a hard time processing what just happened. "Jesus Christ!" he exclaims. "Since when were we invaded by aliens?"

The staff sergeant looks a bit surprise by the question. "What are you talking about?"

"Are you kidding me?! That was a fucking flying saucer!" Matt exclaims.

"Yeah, but that's no alien … Where have you been for the past five years?" Palmer asks.

"What's the date today?" Matt asks.

"November second."

Matt clarifies his question. "I mean, what year?"

Palmer looks at him and smiles for the first time. "What kind of question is that? Have you been living under a rock?"

"Please, just tell me," Matt pleads. "I'm having one of those senior moments."

"2022," Palmer finally answers.

Matt holds his head in disbelief. "I'm fucked."

"Yeah, well we're all fucked," the soldier adds.

While Palmer is driving, Matt looks out the window and sees all the abandoned cars and trucks on the side of the road. There are visible scars of devastation on some of the buildings—damaged concrete walls and broken windows. The infrastructure of the roads, overpasses, and walkways are falling apart, exposing stripped steel skeletons.

Forty minutes later, they approach the military air base, which Matt knows as Burbank Airport. The wrecked Humvee stops at the west Empire Avenue gate before one of the guards opens the security fence. Five other armored military vehicles are leaving the air base as the Humvee enters.

Matt is disturbed about everything he is seeing. There are unusual-looking tanks, antiaircraft cannons, and other military equipment everywhere. There is a lot of activity around the base. Every soldier that passes by looks stressed and agitated.

As they drive by one of many hangars, Matt sees six of the unusual fighter jets parked inside. The retired pilot can finally have a good peek at them. At first sight, the aircraft share some similar features with the F-35 Lightning II, but the fuselage is wider with twin engines instead of one, and the wingspan looks too short to produce lift. The most defined aspect of the fighter jet is two half-shaped capsule cases mounted side by side on top of the fuselage.

Palmer stops the Humvee. "Let's go."

With that, they get out and walk in the hangar. "Wait here," Staff Sergeant adds.

An alarm sounds off from the hangar, and three fighter jets are taxiing out to the runway. Matt is thoroughly intrigued with the aircraft. All three aircraft are pointing down their thrust-vectoring nozzles and take off vertically using a very short space.

Behind Matt, a military officer in his forties is approaching. On the collar of his uniform, a colonel's ranking is displayed. He's talking on his smartphone. "I'll call you back," the colonel says abruptly before hanging up.

The staff sergeant salutes his commanding officer, and they exchange a few words. Still watching the fighter jets flying away, the ex-pilot hears footsteps behind him and assumes that it's Palmer coming back.

"Where does this aircraft come from?" Matt asks curiously.

"Area 51," a familiar voice answers. It's not Palmer.

Matt turns around and can't believe his eyes. "Daniel?"

His best friend, ten years older, is standing in front of him with a smile.

"Man," Matt says, "you have no idea how happy I am to see you." He is still astonished by the sight of his friend.

Both men hug.

"God, I've missed you, Matt!" Daniel says. He looks at Palmer and nods. "Thank you, Staff Sergeant. Good job! That will be all."

"Thanks for saving my life," Matt says to the staff sergeant with gratitude.

"You bet … Stay out of trouble." Palmer salutes them before walking away.

Daniel turns to Matt. "Jesus Christ, look at you! Didn't change a bit and still wearing the same clothes. Un-fucking believable!"

Daniel has a receding hairline and a few more wrinkles on his face. He notices Matt staring at him and rubs his hand across his balding head. "Yeah, I know. I'm losing my hair … that sucks," Daniel says.

"Yeah." The small talk with his friend helps Matt forget for a moment what he has just been through. For the first time since his arrival in this future timeline, he feels safe.

"Man! Everything happened so fast that night," Daniel says. "When you told me about that time machine shit, I have to admit, I thought for a second you'd lost it. I wasn't sure what to believe … and here you are."

Matt looks around and doesn't like what he sees. "What the hell happened here?" he eagerly asks.

"Long story short—this is all due to a perfect storm of excessive warfare, total economic collapse, and the increasing devastation from natural disasters … I'm telling you, Mother Earth is angry. The country has never been so divided since the last civil war. Martial law is enforced in most states. One-half of the military still defends and protects the US Constitution for the people, but the other half serves the interest of the corporations and the government." Daniel takes a deep breath and looks around. "Everybody was wondering when the *big one* would hit California … Well, it happened five years ago."

After what Daniel had just told him, all of Matt's concern is redirected to his sweetheart. "Where's Kayla?"

"Don't worry; she's fine," Daniel assures him. "But she's not living in LA anymore."

Matt is not satisfied with the answer. "Where is she?"

"Safe up north in Oregon." Daniel pauses for a second. "You were right. They went after her."

Matt doesn't like the sound of it. "I want to see her."

"Yeah, I know. I'll take you to her but later. We have a lot to talk about." Daniel pats his friend on the back, and they both walk toward the hangar. "Guess who's the US president."

Thousands of Miles Away in an Underground Military Base

IN THE COMMAND CONTROL ROOM, a military officer is on the phone. "I'm afraid I have bad news, Mr. President. One Vril is down, and the target got away with the Resistance."

White House, Oval Office

PRESIDENT WAIZER IS ON THE phone and is furious. "It is imperative that you find him. I want a team commission 24/7 to scan all military bases in the area and search for any suspicious activity. Use all satellites, drones, and resources available at your disposal. Is that clear?"

"Yes, sir. Understood," the military officer replies.

"Good." Karl hangs up the phone, still enraged by the news.

Burbank, Military Air Base

IN THE HANGAR, MATT IS sitting in the cockpit of one of the unusual-looking fighter jets; the ex-pilot feels right at home in his comfort zone. With Daniel's help, Matt was able to get caught up with information about the sixth-generation fighter aircraft.

"It's a F-37 Peregrine, named after a falcon species that is the fastest member of the animal kingdom. The aircraft is a hybrid between supercruise jet engines and an antigravitational force technology." Matt climbs down from the Peregrine cockpit as Daniel adds, "I'm telling you, this baby makes the old AV-8 Harrier and the F-35 Lightning II look like dinosaurs."

"I'd like to see that for myself." Matt changes the subject to something he has been wondering since he reunited with his buddy. "By the way, how did you find me?"

"Well, you didn't exactly leave quietly that night. It was more like a big bang. They never found your body in what was left of the site after the explosion, so I figured that maybe it was a sign that somehow you made it by using the time machine. The million-dollar question was: where were you? When they ran your ID through the computer archives and I knew it was you, I had a mandate to bring you safely back here at the base."

Matt has a lot of questions to ask his friend, but one is still unanswered. "We were attacked by flying saucers. Where the hell did they come from?"

Daniel looks and admires the F-37. "Same place

where this baby came from—Area 51. After the total economic collapse, people who were employed there started leaking classified technological information to the public. Thanks to YouTube, the truth came out about those flying saucers," he explains.

"Were they developed from alien technology?" Matt asks.

"Not exactly … it's from Germany."

This is the last thing Matt expected to hear and now he is more confused than ever. "What!?"

"Yeah, talk about German engineering … Anyway, the saucer type you saw is the latest Vril generation of aircraft."

"Vril? What is that?" Matt asks.

"It's the code name used for those saucer shaped aircrafts that inherited its technology from the Haunebu Project." Daniel adds.

Matt recalls first hearing about this conspiracy theory project from Kayla when they were at the restaurant. "Haunebu Project? You mean the same one my *surrogate* grandfather was involved with?"

Daniel smiles, already knowing that what's next will blow his friend's mind. "Yep! Viktor Schauberger was not just involved with it; he was the founder of the Haunebu Project. In Nazi Germany, he designed an electromagnetic engine and used it to propel the first flying saucer ever recorded."

This story sounds too outlandish to be true and is raising more questions for Matt. "Then why didn't the Nazis use them in air combat during World War II?"

"From what I've heard, the early prototype saucers were not very stable and didn't perform well in air combat. The objective was more to perfect a long-range bomber," Daniel answers.

Matt grabs his head in disbelief. "That's insane! How could they have hidden a secret like that for all those years?"

Daniel has a simple answer for his friend. "The information about it has been around for a while on the Internet, but without any solid evidence, it's hard to prove facts from fiction." He adds, "When the government and powerful corporations are the puppeteers who control covert information, then they can obviously also conceal the truth from the public."

"What you just said feels too close to home," Matt notes. "If it would not have been for Waizer's desperation to get his hands on my dad's missing data, I wouldn't have ever known about all this." Matt pauses as he looks around. "That's messed up."

After everything Matt has heard, it sounds like the most logical explanation of the technology he worked with at the Waizer lab was that it originated from the Haunebu Project.

"I hate to say this," Matt continues, "but if all that

you're telling me is true, there is actually a chance that the Nazi scientist could be my grandfather."

Daniel nods and has more to tell to his friend about his family history, but that will have to wait. "I don't think those saucers were in the neighborhood by accident," he remarks.

An unpleasant feeling of anxiety surfaces in Matt. "You think they were after me?"

"Yeah, I'm afraid so. I don't know how they found out, but—"

"I think I know," Matt says, interrupting him. "I saw a security camera in the lab … Damn it!" He quickly grabs the time device over his sleeve. "I can't stay here! The only person I can think of who would know about the time device is Karl Waizer. He's going to come after me."

Daniel knows too well that as the president of the United States, Karl has the power and resources to find Matt, but he is determined to not let that happened.

"It's okay, you're safe here with me," Daniel assures his friend.

"No, everybody here is in danger now because of me. Waizer is not going to stop until he gets this."

Matt pulls up his left sleeve. Daniel has always wondered what a time machine would look like, but as he takes a glance at it, he appears a bit disappointed. He didn't really know what to expect, but he certainly imagined it to be something more impressive.

"That's it?" he questions. "That's the time device you used to get here?"

"Yeah, but I also need—" Matt stops short of finishing his sentence, as he is gets carried away in his thoughts.

"What?" Daniel asks.

"I think I have a way to get out of here," Matt says with conviction.

Daniel is perplexed about how his friend plans to pull this off. "How?"

"I'm gonna need your help, buddy," Matt says.

Chapter 10

Burbank, Military Air Base
9:05 p.m. Year 2022

DANIEL AND MATT ARE BOARDING a jet version of the V-22 Osprey aircraft equipped with antigravitational force technology. Twelve soldiers plus Staff Sergeant Palmer are inside the troop transport. The back door closes, and the Osprey takes off vertically.

The aircraft rapidly ascends to high altitude and flies through dark skies over the San Fernando Valley, back to Northridge. It is a short distance by air between the two locations.

When they arrive at their destination, a searchlight mount under the aircraft turns on and starts scanning down below. It continues to fly at low altitude over the abandoned Costco warehouse, heading toward the parking lot. Inside the Osprey, Matt is standing just behind the pilot and sees what he is looking for.

"Over there!" Matt points out.

The searchlight is turned toward what appears to be the flying saucer crash site. The aircraft circles around a few times before the pilot begins to descend for the landing.

Two minutes later, the Osprey touches down not too far from the crash site. Everybody exits the aircraft and immediately runs toward the saucer. Two soldiers are carrying cutting torches and gas tanks. They climb onto the saucer and start cutting the canopy locks. Palmer aims his assault rifle at the metallic canopy already covered with numerous bullet holes and gives the signal.

"Open it," he orders.

A soldier pulls the rescue release handle, and the canopy opens. The pilot and copilot are found dead inside, and the soldiers quickly remove their bodies.

"Clear!" Palmer says.

Matt and Daniel get into the flying saucer cockpit

and look at the instruments. The setup looks surprisingly like a modern fighter jet.

"All right! Here we go!" Matt says.

He turns on the power switch, and all the monitor displays are activated.

"Holy shit!" Daniel says with excitement.

Matt selects the engine setup and scrolls down on the touch screen until he finds what he's looking for. "Bingo!" The screen monitor shows the diagram of two big electromagnetic Tesla coils located in the lower section of the saucer hull. "I need those Tesla coils," Matt says as he points at the screen.

"Do you think that's gonna work?" Daniel asks with a bit of apprehension.

Matt does not have a lot of options at this point. "The same kind of Tesla coil motors brought me here … It's worth a try."

Daniel looks up at the dark skies. "It's not safe to stay in the open like this. We might attract too much attention."

"I agree."

"I'll call the base to send us a crane. The warehouse will make a good shelter," Daniel adds. "What do you need?

Matt thinks for a second as he reviews the Tesla coils' database on the dash screen. "I'm gonna need a boost. I need the biggest power generator you can get me."

"You got it!" Daniel says as he pats his friend on the shoulder. "There's still time to change your mind … Are you sure you don't want to stay here?"

Matt doesn't have any second thoughts. "You know I can't. I'm responsible for this mess. I have to go back and fix it."

Daniel nods and stands up out of the cockpit to address the troop. "All right, guys, listen up! This is Major Matthew Schauberger. He is now in charge of a highly important scientific experiment, and I want you to listen to him carefully."

"A nice hot cup of coffee would be nice. It's gonna be a long night," Matt says to himself before taking a deep breath. He gets out of the saucer cockpit and takes command of the operation.

When the truck with the crane arrives, Matt instructs the operator to lift and move the flying saucer to a the new location. Four Costco forklifts are in place in the warehouse to support the flying saucer fifteen feet in the air. Earlier, the same saucer destroyed a portion of the roof. The destruction now provided an opening for the crane operator to carefully lower down the aircraft though the gap.

As soon as the saucer is secured in place on the forklifts, four soldiers are assigned the task of using blowtorches to open the wrecked engine housing and remove the lowest Tesla coil motor located under the aircraft. The Costco building is loaded with supplies that can be used. Four other soldiers are taking apart the industrial shelves' metal frames to build a support that will be used to anchor the lowest Tesla coil motor in place on the concrete floor. The remaining soldiers are building a twenty-foot walkway ramp, also using the industrial shelves' metal frames. Meanwhile, Daniel and Palmer are helping the troops, as well as supervising the progress of the whole operation. And while all of this is going on, Matt is sitting in the saucer cockpit working on data reconfiguration for the Tesla coils RPM and pulse frequency.

In the middle of the night, an eighteen-wheeler truck arrives. Chained to a flatbed trailer is a massive power generator. They use one-inch electric cables to link it with the saucer's power generator. The soldiers are determined to make good progress through the night.

In the morning, the lowest Tesla coil is already imbedded in the support under the flying saucer. The layout of the gateway is different than the original one from the lab. For practical reasons, Matt decides to keep the highest Tesla coil in the engine bay. As a result, the setup is rotated ninety degrees.

After completing his task with the reconfiguration of the Tesla coil, Matt exits the saucer cockpit. He looks around and is satisfied with the progress. A lot of work has been done, but there's still a lot more to do. He yawns and stretches his arms up in the air. His sleeve falls back revealing half of a carbon fiber case. Suddenly, Matt is reminded of the damaged time device strapped to his forearm and feels a bit uneasy. He turns it on, and a blue screen with error codes is still being displayed. He looks around for Daniel and finds him busy welding a metal section on the ramp nearby.

Matt climbs down the saucer and walks up to him. "Do you have a minute?"

"Yeah, what's up?" Daniel says as he takes off his welding mask.

"I need to talk to Kayla."

Daniel looks anxious. "Calling her is not a good idea. I'm sure they are monitoring all communications by now."

"You don't understand. She has something that I need in order to make the trip possible," Matt explains.

Daniel has to think about it for a moment before saying, "All right … do you think they can finish the job without you?"

Matt takes a deep breath as he looks at the Tesla coils. "Yeah, I don't think they need us here to finish the rest of the job."

"Okay, I'll put Palmer in charge during our absence. We'll have to go back to the base." With a crooked little smile, he adds, "I know how we can get to Oregon quickly."

Chapter 11

Burbank, Military Air Base
10:25 a.m.

ON THE RUNWAY, TWO F-37 Peregrines are ready for takeoff. Matt is sitting in one of the aircraft and has a big smile on his face as he looks at his friend through the canopy glass.

"Now you're talking!" he says to Daniel through his headset microphone.

Daniel switches his radio channel and communicates, "T1 Airfield, WCD-202, 206 ready for takeoff."

"WCD-202, 206 you're clear for takeoff," the airfield controller confirms.

Both Peregrines accelerate fast and take off within a very short distance. They gain altitude and head to Oregon.

At the same time, at an altitude high above the military air base, a stealth drone is spying on them.

At 35,000 feet, both F-37s fly in formation side by

side. Daniel's Peregrine rolls upside down and then slides sideways above Matt's fighter jet. Daniel pushes hard on the control stick and the dual throttle control. As if defying the laws of physics, the aircraft, while inverted, lifts straight up into the sky with amazing acceleration.

"Whoa! That's a new one!" Matt remarks with thrilling enthusiasm.

"You haven't seen anything yet!" Daniel says, still climbing.

Matt knocks on the dashboard and says, "All right, let's see what you can do."

He pushes hard on the dual throttle control and pulls back the control stick. Matt's F-37 lifts off in the sky and in no time catches up with his friend, all with barely pulling g-forces.

Oregon State, Countryside

AMID THE SCENIC AND QUIET countryside, a woman is walking in a vineyard with her German shepherd, Toby. It is Kayla, now ten years older. The dog starts to bark at the roaring sounds of the two fighter jets approaching her location. Both aircraft fly over Kayla before landing in her backyard. Usually, Daniel comes to visit her by himself, so she's curious to see who's flying the second aircraft. Kayla and Toby run to meet the visitors.

Daniel and Matt climb out of their Peregrines. Kayla holds her dog by the collar. The German shepherd is barking and ready to attack.

"It's okay! They're friends. Good boy!" Kayla says to Toby. She can't believe her eyes when she spots Matt and starts to cry. "Oh my God! It's you!"

They both run toward each other and deeply embrace as if a miracle has just happened.

"I'm so sorry, baby, for everything that I've put you through," Matt says with teary eyes.

"I'm just glad you're alive. After what you told me that night, in my heart, I always had faith that you would find a way to come back to me. And here you are. God, I've missed you so much." She kisses Matt and gently rests her head against his chest.

When Daniel arrives closer to them, she holds his hand with gratitude. "I'll be in the backyard. You guys need some time to catch up," Daniel says before heading back to his F-37 with the dog.

Kayla and Matt both give a nod and then walk to the house.

Washington, DC, White House

KARL WAIZER IS WORKING AT his desk in the Oval Office when the phone rings.

"This is the president."

Underground Military Base

IN A COMMAND CONTROL ROOM, a military officer is on the phone while looking at satellite footage of two aircraft parked behind a house. The spy camera zooms in on Matt and Daniel but cannot identify their faces.

"Sir, we detected suspicious activity with two F-37 aircraft that departed from Burbank Air Base and just landed in Willamette Valley, Oregon."

Karl takes a moment to think before giving his orders. "Send a tactical team to the site immediately for further investigation."

"Yes, sir! Right away, sir," the officer replies before hanging up the phone.

Oregon State, Countryside

BACK IN THE HOUSE AT the vineyard, Matt is sitting on the couch in the living room drinking some homemade lemonade. Kayla is walking up the stairs from the basement, carrying a box labeled with the name *Cedric Schauberger*.

"Remember this?" she asks.

Matt walks up to her. "Yeah, let me help you." He takes the box from Kayla and places it on the coffee table. "I can't believe you kept this box with you all this time."

"Well, I know you never wanted to open your dad's old boxes, but I found a lot of interesting things in them." Kayla opens the box and pulls out a handful of photos. She pulls out a black-and-white photograph that is familiar to him. It is the same one they found earlier in the restaurant from the conspiracy theory website that shows Viktor Schauberger; his father, Cedric; and one of the Nazi officers who lookalike Matt all standing together. "Look what I found. This is the original," Kayla notes.

Matt takes the photo and looks at it. "Oh … the family picture."

They both sit down on the couch. "This picture is dated November 9, 1944. Take a look on the other side," she says.

Matt looks in the back of the picture, where all the

names of the people in the photo are written down. He can't believe what he's reading. Right under the name *Hans Müller*, Matt's name is written and then followed by a question mark. In the same way, his father's name is written under the name *Stefan Heinrich*.

"Did you write this?" he asks.

"No, it wasn't me. It had to be your dad. Now, look at the name of the other Nazi officer," Kayla adds.

Matt looks at the name list and sees the name *Herbert Waizer* written. He turns the photo around and looks at the Nazi officer's face. As he carefully examines the photo, he recognizes some features of a younger Herbert, likely in his midtwenties. "No way!" Matt gasps. "That old son of a bitch was a Nazi … Why am I not surprised?"

"Your dad did some serious background research on Hans Müller and Stefan Heinrich."

While Kayla is busy pulling a pile of documents out of the box, Matt stares at the photo with his father and the Nazi officer who looks like him. "Were you able to find any other information of what could have happened my dad?"

Kayla gives another picture to Matt. In the photo, there is a striking resemblance between Cedric and Matt as they stand in the background behind a group of German soldiers. "This picture was taken a week after the other one on November 16, 1944. These two pictures are the only evidence we have that your dad is alive in that time period."

"What do you know about Hans Müller?" Matt asks.

Kayla suddenly feels nervous and looks at the picture that Matt is holding. "I was afraid you'd ask that … I know Müller is not in this picture," she answers cautiously.

Matt looks at her in disbelieve. "So, is that me in the photo?"

Kayla nods her head slowly. "Most likely. Müller was already dead by the time this picture was taken."

Matt stands up and holds his head as if he needs to come up with something quickly. "After Cooper was assassinated, I gave up the idea of using the time machine to find my dad. He used to say the universe works in mysterious ways. Even if I go back in my present time and try to prevent Cooper's murder, there's no evidence here that I will succeed. The only thing I know is I will somehow end up in this picture. Maybe it's a sign."

"Maybe, but I don't like where you're going with this," Kayla says.

"This picture is proof that I will find him. I know what to do now."

Kayla jumps off the couch. "What!? No! Have you lost your mind?"

Matt gently holds her arms. "No! It's all becoming

clear to me. Look at it," he says, showing her the picture. "It's obvious that I was there … or will be there."

Kayla raises her voice as she starts to become anxious about Matt's plan. "Damn you! You're talking about going in to Nazi Germany here! Of all the places in the world, why does it have to be Nazi Germany?"

"I don't like the idea either, but please trust me on this one. I know I can find him with your help and all the information my dad has left behind."

Matt feels confident with his plan and is strangely at ease with it. Seeing that he has some clarity about the situation, Kayla starts to calm down. "I know how much your dad means to you, but this is suicide … You're crazy."

Matt just looks at her, waiting for an approval.

"I know you would do the same for me if my life was in danger," Kayla says in a surrendering tone.

"I'd do it in a heartbeat!" Matt gently takes her in his arms and passionately kisses her as they embrace.

"I've missed you so much," Kayla tells him. "For the past ten years, this picture has been haunting me. I thought you might have been trapped in the past … and now here you are."

A feeling of remorse starts to rise within Matt, which triggers a haunting thought. "I should have listened to you and never taken that job. I'm so sorry for everything I have put you through."

"Don't go. Stay with me," she pleads with him.

"I can't. Karl Waizer knows I'm here."

Kayla is suddenly terrified. "But how?"

"When I entered this time through the lab, I was caught on a security camera … I wouldn't be here without Daniel's intervention."

It doesn't take long for Kayla to realize the gravity of the situation. "He wants the time machine."

Matt nods his head in agreement. "Because of me, you and Daniel are not safe anymore."

As Kayla prepares to say good-bye to her sweetheart for a second time, not knowing if she will ever see him again, her heart is consumed with a mix of fear and hope. "Promise me you will find your dad and come back to me, because I don't want to go through this again."

"I promise." Matt kisses her and adds, "Please tell me you still have the flash drive I gave you."

Kayla smiles at him. "Come with me."

They both head down to the basement. She opens the door of a big Liberty safe. Stored in it are guns, assault rifles, ammunition, and military gear that would not normally be in the possession of a civilian.

"Jesus! You don't mess around," Matt exclaims.

"This was Daniel's idea for self-protection." Kayla pulls out a picture of her and Matt and retrieves the USB flash drive from behind the frame. "Here it is!" she says as she hands him the flash drive.

Matt breathes a sigh of relief. "Thanks! May I use your computer?"

"Of course."

He walks to a nearby computer, pulls up his sleeve, and takes off the time device. Matt then sets up a workstation and gets down to business.

Kayla is intrigued when she sees the time device. "So this is the time machine that brought you here? It doesn't look like much."

"Yes, but this is only one part of it."

Matt is downloading a recovery program from the flash drive and begins an error checklist on the time device.

"How does this work?" Kayla asks.

"Other than the time option, it functions like a GPS navigation system. I have only tested it in the lab … Well, and one time in the corridor, but in theory, it allows me to go anywhere in time."

"Like Nazi Germany?" Kayla adds with a bit of sarcasm.

"Yeah … but to make this trip possible, it also requires the opening of a gateway, and that's the tricky part. The Resistance shot down one of the saucer-shaped aircraft, and the engine turns out to be exactly what I need," Matt explains.

"Sounds complicated. I think a flying DeLorean would have been less trouble."

"Tell me about it!" Matt resets and reboots the system on the time device. He is staring at the flat screen and anxiously waiting for any kind of response. "Come on!"

A moment later, the time device screen turns on, and everything comes back to normal. Matt releases a long sigh of relief. "Thank you." He then turns his attention to Kayla. "Babe, what do you know about that Müller guy?"

Matt, Kayla, and Daniel are all sitting on the couch going over Matt's plan of action. The dog is resting his head on Daniel's lap. From the box, Kayla picks up a photocopy of an old German newspaper article and a picture of a Nazi officer and gives them to Matt. At first sight, the man in the picture looks like he could be mistaken for Matt.

"This is Hans Müller," Kayla says.

Daniel comes closer to take a better peek at the photo. "Yeah, he does kind of look like you."

Matt also looks at the picture while Kayla reads the headlines from the newspaper. "*Hauptmann Hans Müller, missing since November 9, 1944. He was last seen in the morning in Xanten, 19 kilometers from Rheinberg Air Base where he was scheduled to report at 6:30 a.m. the same day.*"

"Apparently, he died the same day this the family

picture was taken," Matt points out. "But I'm obviously the one who is in it, not him."

Kayla gives Matt a printed copy of a Google Map that was also in the box. The map shows a German road with a red mark indicating the longitude and latitude where Hans Müller's body was found. "His body was found one month later at the bottom of a cliff right there," Kayla says as she points to the red marking on the map.

"How did he die?" Matt asks.

"I don't know. There's no information about this."

"It's a long shot, but if I can get myself to this place where he died, then I can use his identity." Matt pulls up his sleeve and enters the location coordinates data of the spot on the map into the time device.

Meanwhile, in the vineyard, a tactical team of six men discreetly head toward Kayla's house. A soldier looks through his riflescope and aims at one of the windows. He can see Matt.

"Positive target ID," the soldier says into high-tech Bluetooth headset.

A moment later, one of the winery employees walks out of the garage and spots a soldier in the field. The soldier takes aim with his suppressor-equipped rifle and kills the man.

Inside the house, the dog starts to bark in a very aggressive way and runs to the front door. Daniel draws his Sig 9mm handgun from his holster and cautiously opens the front door. "Are you expecting anyone?" he asks Kayla.

"No," she replies apprehensively.

The dog runs out to the front porch and continues to bark loudly. Suddenly, Toby starts to cry in pain after a slight whistle from a bullet is heard. Kayla stands up. Matt and Daniel quickly realize they are under attack.

"Get down!" both men cry out.

Matt jumps on Kayla to cover her before pulling her down to the floor, but it's too late. A bullet has already passed through the window and hit Kayla in the chest. A second later, machine guns are blasting at the house and shattering all the windows.

Panic-stricken, Matt turns Kayla's body to face him. "Kayla! Kayla!" he desperately calls out.

She is unconscious and bleeding heavily from her chest. Matt then briefly looks over at his friend with a frightened look. Amid the chaos, Daniel witnesses the tragic scene and becomes enraged as he sees Kayla lying on the floor, lifeless.

"Fuck!" he screams.

Daniel runs to the basement and opens the Liberty safe. He takes out two assault rifles, an ammunition pouch, and a tactical belt loaded with grenades. He rushes back to the living room and calls out to his friend. "Matt!"

Daniel throws an assault rifle to him, along with two grenades. He then continues to shoot back through the windows with his assault rifle before taking out two other grenades from the pouches. He looks at his friend. "Ready? Now!"

Daniel and Matt each pull out the safety pin from his grenade. They quickly throw them out through the windows before taking cover on the floor. In the front yard of the house, the grenades blow up, and the tactical team runs for cover.

Back in the living room, Kayla slowly opens her eyes in pain.

"Baby, hang on!" Matt says desperately. "I'm going to get you out of here."

"No … go … save your dad. I love—" With that, Kayla takes her last breath.

Tears of pain and anger overwhelm Matt as he watches her eyes close. "No! No! Kayla, don't!" Matt begs as he continues to shake her, hoping that she will somehow open her eyes again.

Daniel throws out a few smoke grenades and takes a quick look at her lifeless body. "I'm so sorry, Matt. She's gone." He grabs Matt by the shoulder. "We have to go now! C'mon, let's go!" Daniel orders him.

Matt gently lays Kayla down on the floor. He looks at her one last time before Daniel pulls him up, and they both run out to the backyard.

Daniel throws more smoke grenades along their way, keeping the tactical team shooting blind. The men climb into their fighter jets and quickly start the engines. Numerous bullets fly at them. Matt and Daniel take off and open fire through the smoke cloud, using the 20mm machine gun built in under the aircraft nose. The burst of rapid fire has a devastating effect, leaving no survivors among the tactical team.

"Let's get out of here," Daniel says as he pushes forward the dual-throttle control. Both Peregrines accelerate and climb rapidly to high altitude, heading back to Los Angeles.

Chapter 12

Washington DC, White House

IN THE OVAL OFFICE, THREE generals and an admiral are in a meeting. Karl is on the phone and looks very upset. "How did he get away?" Karl asks furiously.

"The tactical team was overpowered, sir. The target escaped with one accomplice identified as Col. Daniel Myers. They left no survivors," the officer says nervously.

"Where are they now?" Karl asks.

"I have on radar two aircraft heading south, most likely back to Burbank Air Base," the officer answers.

Karl hangs up and thinks for a second before he stands up to face his guests. "Gentlemen, I was just informed of an imminent terrorist attack. The target has been identified as Matthew Schauberger. He is a domestic terrorist who murdered my father. He is on his way to Los Angeles as we speak and has in his possession a WMD."

All three generals and the admiral suddenly look deeply worried about the disturbing news.

Pacific Ocean

AN AIRCRAFT CARRIER IS AT sea with flying saucers on the flight deck. On the bridge, the phone rings, and an officer answers. "Bridge." The officer hands the phone over to his superior. "Captain, incoming call for you."

The man in charge takes the phone. "Captain Maxwell speaking," he says.

The captain's facial expression becomes one of disbelief as he listens to the order from the White House.

"You can't be serious! All right. I understand."

The captain hangs up the phone and picks up the radio communication handset to address the ship's crew members. "All hands prepare for battle."

The crew on the flight deck is on alert, and flying saucers immediately begin taking off.

Ventura County Airspace

ALONG THE PACIFIC COAST, BOTH fighter jets are flying in formation at high speed over the clouds. Matt is feeling devastated, and Daniel is worried about his friend.

"Are you hanging in there?" Daniel asks delicately.

"She's dead because of me," Matt says. He is clearly filled with guilt.

"No, it's not your fault. I should have known better and been more careful. I know it was hard for you to leave her, but—"

Both men are interrupted by the incoming missile sound alert.

"Incoming! Evasive maneuvers!" Daniel exclaims before switching his radio transmission to communicate with the control tower back at the air base. "T1 airfield, this is WCD-202. We are under attack! Request for air support!"

"Roger that! Hang in there, 202. Help is on the way," the controller answers.

The F-37s bank hard and release several flares. Two missiles heading toward them explode in the burst of flares.

"Shit! That was close!" Daniel diverts his attention for a second to his friend. "Matt! I need you to focus right now! Are you okay?"

"Yeah! I got your six!"

"Good! That's my boy!"

A formation of flying saucers is coming from the west.

"Visual contact, six bogeys, two o'clock coming fast—" Matt says. But before he can finish his sentence, one of the flying saucers accelerates to an incredible speed and stops just a few feet away from Matt's F-37. "Jesus!" he screams out.

"Dive! Dive! We have to bring them closer to the ground level. That's going to stop them from jumping on us," Daniel says as he pushes hard on the dual-throttle control.

Both fighter jets dive in an evasive maneuver, but the saucers follow and launch four more missiles at them. The alarms sound off.

"Incoming!" Matt yells.

Escaping from the line of fire, both pilots pull back their control sticks and level their aircraft just twenty feet over the Pacific Coast Highway. They release more flares at the four approaching missiles to confuse their guidance system. The weapons change course and explode in the decoys proximity, right behind the two fighter jets.

"Follow me!" Daniel says.

The friends are flying their Peregrines at a very low altitude above the winding highway. The saucers flying above are following them from a higher altitude.

"Stay as low as possible and keep going to Santa Monica. The urban environment will be our best protection. Our Peregrines are no match for their speed, but we are smaller and more nimble," Daniel briskly explains.

When they arrive in Santa Monica, Daniel makes a quick turn down a side street and makes a 180-degree turn to face one of the flying saucers. Two EMP missiles are launched from his F-37, aiming straight at the saucer and breaking through its force field. Daniel switches on the control stick for the machine gun trigger and blasts the saucer with bullets. The saucer violently crashes into a building.

Meanwhile, two saucers are tailing Matt and shooting at him. "God damnit!" he yells. "All right! You guys want to play hard? Let's play!"

Matt flies his F-37 under an overpass of the 10 Freeway. The saucer shoots at the overpass and destroys it. After clearing the other side, Matt then steers his fighter jet straight up in the air and makes an inverse loop. One of the saucers is right on his target, and Matt takes the shot. The saucer explodes and falls out of control, but the fight is not over yet. Matt sees another formation of eight saucers coming fast. "Shit!" Matt talks to his friend through the radio communication. "Dan, we have more company!"

Daniel looks at his radar. "I see them!"

Matt catches up with Daniel, and they are ready to fight against the aggressors. Realizing they are outnumbered, Daniel's adrenaline goes through the roof as he sees them coming. "Bring it on, bitches!" he screams out.

They both fly their aircraft at high speed, just over the cars on the street. What they don't realize is that they're heading straight into a trap. At the end of the street, a saucer pulls out from nowhere. It stops right in front of Matt and Daniel, ready to discharge a death ray. Before the saucer can properly aim, a third friendly F-37 comes to the rescue and fires two EMP missiles at it. The death ray shoots from the saucer and hits and destroys Matt's F-37 left vertical stabilizer, but the aircraft is able to take the impact and continue to fly. Both pilots look at each other with relief as they see ten Peregrines coming their way.

"Yeah, baby! That's what I'm talking about!" Daniel says enthusiastically.

All ten F-37s engage the fight against the saucers as they break formation.

"Now this is more like a fair fight," Daniel jokingly comments. His excitement quickly turns to anxiety as he realizes President Waizer's obsession will not stop until he gets his hands on the time device, even if it means killing everyone standing in his way. Daniel now fears for Matt's safety and makes the decision not to go back to the air base in case the security has been compromised in any way.

"I have to get you out of here before it gets worse," Daniel said to Matt. "Follow me!"

"We can't leave them in the middle of a fight."

"This is not your call to make, Matt. Let's go!" Daniel says to him with an unusual authoritarian tone in his voice.

Matt complies with Daniel, and the two pilots change course, heading northeast. Daniel doesn't like what is coming next and takes a deep breath before saying, "This is it, Matt! It's time to say farewell."

"What are you talking about?" Matt asks, clearly confused.

"I want you to go to the warehouse. This is your chance to leave this place. I'll stay up here to keep the sky clear … Good luck, buddy!" Daniel says.

"Negative! I'm not leaving you," Matt insists.

"Leave now! That's an order, Soldier!" Daniel

salutes his friend before he pulls the control stick and flies upward.

"Thank you, my friend." Matt pushes the dual throttle control to supercruise and heads to the warehouse. It takes less than two minutes to reach his destination, and he lands the F-37 in the Costco parking lot. He jumps out of the aircraft cockpit and rushes in the warehouse. Palmer comes to meet him. "Is everything ready?" Matt asks.

"Yes, sir!"

"Great! Thank you, Staff Sergeant. I need the power generator ready on my signal."

"You got it!" Palmer goes and takes his position at the flatbed trailer.

As Matt runs to the flying saucer, he looks up through the broken roof of the warehouse and sees Daniel's F-37 flying by, patrolling the airspace. He then climbs up a ladder leaning on the edge of the saucer and gets into the cockpit. Without wasting any time, he starts the engines.

Down under the aircraft, both Tesla coils start to spin in opposite directions with increasing speed. Matt watches the operation system on the dashboard screen and sees that everything seems to be working properly. He steps out of the cockpit and gives Palmer the signal to start the power generator. Matt then rushes back to the ladder and climbs down.

Meanwhile, on the saucer's dashboard screen, a warning sign pops up as the Tesla coils exceed 12,000 RPM. A tracking system has been activated.

Washington, DC, Pentagon

IN A COMMAND CENTER, A military officer is looking at his computer monitor and receives an incoming message in his headset.

"Sir, I just received a signal of an unauthorized engine activation. It's from the Vril's transponder that was shot down yesterday in Northridge," the officer says as he relays the message to the president of the United States.

Karl is standing behind the officer. "It's him ... He's trying to get away," Karl whispers to himself before addressing the officer. "Do you have the position?"

"Yes, sir," the officer replies.

In a desperate attempt to stop Matt, Karl gives his final orders. "Redirect the attack to that location. Now!"

Northridge, in the Warehouse

MATT TURNS ON THE TIME device with the coordinates data of Nazi Germany already programmed in. He steps on the walkway ramp in front of the gateway and gives Palmer the thumbs up.

Half a mile away from the warehouse, a flying

saucer is approaching rapidly. It fires a missile that hits the loading dock section of the Costco. Matt and the soldiers are thrown to the ground from the impact of the explosion.

In his F-37, Daniel can see what is happening below, but he's not in range to stop it. "No!" he screams.

Daniel rolls down his aircraft and dives right at the saucer, firing at it with everything he's got. The saucer is hit hard and explodes in midair.

Back in the warehouse, Matt gets up from the floor and steps back on the walkway ramp. The setup with the Tesla coils is untouched by the explosion, and they are still in motion. As he presses the Enter key on the touch screen, a spark of light from the gateway connects with the metal ball on the time device. Matt starts to run toward it as fast as he can.

Meanwhile, in the sky over the Costco parking lot, another saucer-shaped aircraft appears and aims its death ray at Matt. Not too far away, Daniel changes course and goes after the new threat. Unfortunately, he is out of missiles and without hesitation, he has a fraction of a second to make his next move.

"Good luck, my friend," Daniel says as he bids a final, silent good-bye to Matt.

The saucer shoots at Matt, but Daniel flies his fighter jet in the direct line of fire. His F-37 is hit violently and explodes. The blast pushes the wrecked F-37 into the warehouse. At the same moment, Matt is running for his life toward the gateway as he takes a quick glance over his shoulder, witnessing with horror the ultimate sacrifice his friend had made. He jumps and vanishes into it just before the wrecked fighter jet destroys everything in its path.

Chapter 13

Inside the Gateway

TIME SEEMS TO SLOW DOWN until Matt is perfectly frozen in time. The world around him starts to move backward faster and faster on a massive scale. As the space around him begins to morph to a funnel cloud with rays of light, the time traveler is pulled into it. At the end of the funnel cloud, a light is getting as bright as the sun, and Matt is rushed right through it.

Germany, 1944
6:00 a.m.

A GERMAN SOLDIER IS RIDING his R75 BMW motorbike up a hill along a winding dirt road.

Suddenly, in the middle of the road, about thirty feet in front of him, sparks and rays of light appear out of nowhere. In an attempt to avoid the supernatural phenomena, the soldier swerves and loses control of his motorbike.

At that moment, Matt emerges from the gateway and jumps out of the way. He witnesses the soldier on the motorbike sliding and slamming against a big rock. The rider is ejected from his vehicle, leaving the motorbike lying on the roadside. The German soldier stands up and appears confused. He takes a look at the time traveler and immediately pulls his gun from its holster.

Matt runs toward the soldier, grabs the hand with the gun, and a fight ensues. After a few punches and some wrestling, Matt manages to push the German soldier over the cliff. He checks to see if there is anyone around and then switches off the time device and covers it with his shirt sleeve. He looks down the edge of the cliff and sees the German soldier lying motionless at the bottom.

"Fuck!" he exclaims regretfully.

Matt pulls up the motorcycle and examines it. He opens the two leather saddlebags and finds extra uniforms and a leather flying helmet. He proceeds to hide the motorcycle behind a bush and then climbs down the cliff.

When he gets to the bottom and takes a closer look at the German soldier, he recognizes the face of the dead man as Hans Müller from the photo Kayla had shown him. He searches the body and finds identification papers.

"I killed Hans Müller," Matt says to himself.

As he continues to search the body, Matt finds some money and a valuable document listing where the German soldier was heading, which could help him locate his father. He takes a deep breath before removing the dead man's helmet, goggles, leather jacket, watch, boots, and holster belt. At a nearby river, Matt takes a minute to wash his face. He finally burns his original clothes and buries them before riding off on the motorbike.

Half a mile from an air base, six Messerschmitt Bf 109 fighter airplanes, followed by four Junker bombers, fly low across the tree-lined road. Matt slows down at the checkpoint where four German soldiers are chatting. Upon seeing him, one of the soldiers raises his hand and yells out, "Halt!"

Two soldiers approach and ask for identification. Matt stops and takes out his papers. The soldier looks at him quickly and then nods to the others to let him through. He returns the papers to Matt.

"*Begrüßen Sie die Rheinberg-Basis* (Welcome to Rheinberg Base), *Hauptmann Müller*," the German soldier says.

"*Danke* (Thank you)," Matt replies before continuing on. He rides through the base and turns off his motorbike. He looks around and sees a big airfield, stretching out from both sides of the building. He also spots a control tower. Various types of airplanes are parked. Matt reaches into his coat pocket and pulls out the document. As he reads it through, the last line catches his attention: "*Report to lieutenant Col. Max Ibel at 6:30 a.m.*" Matt looks at his watch and notes that the time is 6:49 a.m. *Shit! I'm late!*

Matt stops the first soldier passing by and asks where can he find Lieutenant Colonel Ibel. The soldier points in the direction of the airfield.

Next to one of the bombers, Matt sees a senior officer in his midforties surrounded by a dozen pilots. He is holding a map and appears to be briefing them on an assignment of some sorts. Matt walks over to them, and before he arrives, all the pilots start to run to their Bf 109 airplanes.

"*He Sie! Sind Sie ein pilot?*" the lieutenant colonel says.

"*Ja Herr.*" Matt gives the document to him. "I'm here to report to Lieutenant Colonel Ibel."

"I'm Colonel Ibel." The high-ranking German

officer quickly reads the letter and gives it back to Matt. "You're late, Hauptmann Müller!"

"I am sorry, sir. I—"

Matt is interrupted by the distant echo of multiple bomb explosions. Meanwhile, not too far from them, a pilot is standing next to a Bf 109. The man is smoking a cigarette and staring at Matt. Matt recognizes his face from the family picture. It is a young, twenty-five-year-old Herbert Waizer. Matt struggles to hide his sudden animosity toward the younger Waizer.

Lieutenant Colonel Ibel has suddenly decided on a different agenda for the pilot. "Your transfer will have to wait, Hauptmann Müller. We need all pilots available. You will accompany Squadron 209 to secure air defense. Is that clear?"

"Yes, sir!" Matt agrees.

Lieutenant Colonel Ibel signals to a young soldier to take Matt to his airplane. "Follow me, sir," the young soldier says.

Matt complies and runs behind him while pulling his leather flying helmet from the saddlebags. As soon as they arrive at the Bf 109 airplane, the young soldier helps Matt with the gear, straps, and parachute bag. He places Matt's saddlebags in a small compartment space behind the cockpit. A big number *8* is printed on the side of the plane. Matt climbs on the wing and gets into the single-seat cockpit.

The young man closes the canopy and says, "Good luck, sir!"

They both salute each other before Matt takes a quick scan of the simplistic dashboard layout. "Not what I had in mind for today," he says to himself as he starts the engine. He then joins twelve other Bf 109 airplanes, including Herbert's, on the runway. They all take off and ascend rapidly to altitude.

The Bf 109s fly in formation toward the enemy airplanes, and it doesn't take long before one of the pilots spots what they are looking for.

"Enemy aircraft at ten o'clock," one of the pilots says in the radio communication.

Matt looks at the horizon and sees sixteen British Royal Air Force (RAF) Spitfire airplanes in formation. "This is not good!" Matt mumbles to himself.

The Bf 109s change course and fly straight at the Spitfires. One of the Bf 109 planes comes up beside Matt's airplane. "What is your name, number 8?" the German pilot asks Matt using the radio communication.

"Müller."

"I'm Oesau, the squadron leader. Müller, you're with Krupps and me!" he says.

"Roger that!" Matt confirms.

Oesau's Bf 109 banks hard right followed by Matt and Krupps. They break the formation and sneak behind the Spitfires. Matt feels uneasy as he follows the squadron leader. All three Bf l09s peel off and trap one of the RAF airplanes. Another Spitfire comes to the rescue of his wingman and goes after Oesau.

"There's one at my four o'clock!" Oesau says.

Matt breaks left and dives to gain speed. "Hang on!"

He sees the Spitfire firing its .303-inch caliber machine guns at Oesau's airplane. Matt closes the circle by turning inwards. The Spitfire is now in his direct line of fire. Matt tries to avoid shooting at the English pilot by aiming at the left wing as he presses on the trigger. A blast of bullets rush out and cut the left wing of the Spitfire in half. The RAF airplane falls from the sky, and the English pilot ejects before the plane crashes. In the meantime, another Spitfire comes up behind Matt and fires five shots into his port wing.

"Number 8, there's one on your six o'clock!" Krupps warns.

Matt anxiously looks over both shoulders from his canopy, trying to catch a glimpse at the Spitfire as the bullet trails are flying at him. "I can't see anything!" He starts rolling in a scissor maneuver but fails to throw off the enemy plane.

"He's still behind you! I'm coming!" Krupps says before changing course.

Another Bf 109 is closer and coming in the opposite direction. "I'll take care of this one," Herbert says with a calm tone of voice.

Matt begins to weave to avoid being shot. "Where is he?" he asks frantically.

Herbert's airplane is now in a collision course with Matt's Bf 109. He stares at Herbert wide-eyed through his windshield as they are about to have a midair collision.

"Break left!" Herbert yells into his headset microphone just before squeezing the trigger.

Matt's Bf 109 is hit in the front windshield and the back vertical antenna. In a quick maneuver, he makes a vertical down roll, leaving a clear shot for Herbert. "Jesus Christ!" Matt exclaims. Herbert takes the shot and flies away, leaving the Spitfire exploding into pieces. Matt is very upset. "Son of a bitch!"

He is still in a dogfight and doesn't have the luxury of time to let his emotion get the best of him. Through heavy snow noise in the radio communication, Matt hears a warning from Oesau. "Look out at seven o'clock!"

Matt makes a steep turn diving down and then pulls back hard on the control stick to ascend. The Spitfire is still on his tail, but it loses speed on the ascent. Matt performs a barrel roll and then moves behind the RAF airplane, which is now in his direct line of fire. But now he's moving too fast in relation to the Spitfire, so he quickly fires and rolls away to avoid a collision.

A trail of bullets pierce the fuselage of the RAF airplane, and it explodes. Matt's airplane is hit by some of the debris but flies away without any serious damage. He checks around for any sign of other Spitfires and sees Krupps's Bf 109 being gunned down and then falling down in flames.

"Jesus! And I thought the saucers were bad!" Matt says to himself while he catches his breath.

After a bloody air combat resulting in wrecked airplanes from both sides falling out of the sky, three remaining Spitfires retreat back to England in full throttle. One Spitfire had been separated from the pack and is still in the fight zone. Matt engages in pursuit toward it, and the crosshairs lock onto the target. As he is about to fire, he remembers who the real enemy is and releases his finger from the trigger. Not too far away, Herbert is upset as he watches Matt passing up an opportunity for a clear shot at the RAF airplane.

A few seconds later, two brand-new German Me 262 fighter jets pass Matt's airplane at high speed and open fire at all three Spitfires. The Spitfires have no chance against the more advanced Me 262, and all three are shot down.

Oesau opens a radio channel. "Mission accomplished," he announces. "Back to the base."

The remaining Bf 109s change course, heading back to the air base, but Herbert flies next to Matt's Bf 109 and opens a radio channel.

"Hauptmann Müller, break formation. You are coming with me," Waizer orders.

"Roger," Matt replies.

Both airplanes break formation and bank to the right, heading south.

Chapter 14

ALMOST RUNNING OUT OF FUEL, Matt and Herbert arrive at their destination. Matt looks down and sees a massive hangar standing in the middle of an open field surrounded by a dense forest.

Lake Constance Base, Airfield

BOTH BF 109S LAND ON the runway and park on the green airfield. Once Matt gets out of his airplane and takes his gear, a maintenance team gets to work to fixing the damaged.

Herbert comes over with a stone-cold face. "You are bad news," he says. "I ended up in that dogfight because you were late, and then you passed on a perfectly clear shot to kill the enemy! Don't let me down again." Herbert turns his back on Matt and starts walking away. "Follow me," Herbert demands with an irritated tone of voice.

"Yes, sir," Matt obediently responds.

Matt follows him to a parked *Kübelwagen*, and they leave the airfield in the military vehicle.

After driving down a bumpy dirt road for fifteen minutes, the men arrive at their destination. Herbert stops the vehicle in front of the biggest hangar Matt has ever seen. Ten years earlier, this had been the birthplace of the most infamous airship of all: the LZ-129 Hindenburg designed and built by the Zeppelin company—the same airship that met her tragic fate in 1937 in Manchester Township, New Jersey. The hangar is now occupied by her twin sister airship, which takes up most of the space inside.

"Wait here," Herbert says.

Matt complies and waits at the entrance, while Herbert walks into the hangar. As he standing there, his eyes catch sight of the gigantic airship parked inside.

"Whoa, that's big!" he whispers to himself in amazement.

As Matt observes the 803-foot long Graf Zeppelin II LZ-130 Hindenburg, a man in his early fifties with a gray beard and wearing a white lab coat walks up behind him.

"Yes, she is indeed … the last of her kind. Isn't she magnificent?" the older man says.

"Yes, she sure is," Matt replies without looking back, distracted by the massive size and beauty of the airship.

"It breaks my heart to witness the end of this airship era … like the untimely death of a beautiful woman. They move with such natural grace and beauty," the man says poetically.

Matt turns around to introduce himself to this eloquent voice behind him. He does a double take when he recognizes the bearded man from the black-and-white family picture.

"By the way, I am Dr. Viktor Schauberger," the man says while offering the new recruit a handshake.

"Pleased to meet you, sir. I'm … I am Hans Müller."

As he gives Matt a handshake, Viktor has a curious look of déjà vu on his face. "Have we met before, Herr Müller?"

"No, I don't think so," Matt quickly replies.

"For a moment, I thought—" Viktor gives him a friendly smile. "Never mind. General Becker speaks highly of you ... and says you are the best among his men for this assignment."

Matt can't help but stare at him. "Were you involved with the construction of this airship?"

Viktor is amused by the pilot inquiry. "No ... I'm part of a different project. I like to think of myself as a pioneer to advance new technology for the future. The *Reichsfuhrer* follows our work closely." Viktor gestures to Matt to head inside the hangar. "Walk with me."

In front of the LZ-130 Hindenburg control car, Herbert is talking with two men in white lab coats. Matt recognizes one of them as his father, Cedric Schauberger. Stunned by the sight of his father, Matt quickly calms himself amid the group in order to not draw any attention. The other man comes forward to speak to Viktor.

"Ah! Herr doctor, would you please join us for a photograph?"

"With pleasure," Viktor says.

Cedric is distracted by Viktor's arrival and is then visibly startled when he sees Matt standing next to him.

One of the scientist calls out, "Come on, everybody."

In disbelief, Cedric loses his balance for a second

and knocks down a welding gas tank on the floor. The loud noise echoes into the hangar.

"Whoa! Be careful!" Herbert exclaims.

"Sorry about that," Cedric says.

He immediately puts the tank back in place and joins Viktor and the other guys for a photograph. A tripod with a camera is already set up for them. Matt is standing in the back with his eyes wide open as he recognizes the familiar set. "The family picture," he whispers to himself.

The photographer settles down behind his camera to take a look through his viewfinder. "Okay, everyone … look this way please."

"One moment!" Viktor interrupts as he looks at Matt. "Please, Herr Müller, join us."

Matt takes off his leather coat, drops his saddlebags, and walks over to the group to stand next to Viktor. The photographer is ready to shoot. The flash dazzles them all.

"Thank you, all!" the photographer says.

Viktor looks at his watch and then turns to the new recruit. "I have to talk to you about your new assignment. Come with me."

Matt and his father make brief eye contact before he leaves the hangar. In an underground bunker next to the hangar, Viktor and Matt head to the chief scientist's office. His desk is buried with documents, and bookshelves cover the walls of his elaborately furnished office. "Please, have a seat," Viktor says politely.

The doctor takes out a document from the drawer and starts to read it. "You graduated first of your class at the Lufftwaffe Academy, and your service for this country as a pilot has been outstanding. Germany needs more patriots like you ... Tell me, Herr Müller, do you believe we will win the war?"

"Yes, sir."

"And how are we going to win with the whole world against us?"

Matt does not like where this discussion is heading. "The Führer will lead us to victory."

"Yes, of course." Viktor gives him an awkward smile of agreement. "But the Führer also needs technological advantages to maintain our superiority. My organization is involved in the development of experimental aircraft. Your assignment is to test one of those aircraft and push it to the limit. Are you up for the challenge, Mr. Müller?"

"Yes, sir," Matt agrees.

"Good ... very good."

"If I may, sir, what kind of aircraft are you referring to?" Matt asks.

Viktor stands up and walks around his desk toward the new recruit. "Let me show you."

In the same underground bunker where they are,

Viktor takes Matt to one of the corridors, which leads them eighty feet under the airship hangar.

"Here we are," the doctor says as they approach a large, rusty metal door. Two soldiers are on duty guarding the restricted area, standing in attention. "Before going any farther, I must remind you once again that everything here is highly classified. Nothing behind this door can ever be revealed to anyone, not even the future Mrs. Müller. Are we clear?"

"Yes, sir."

Viktor looks and nods at one of the two soldiers. Immediately, the soldiers open the door without saying anything. The doctor steps aside and says, "After you."

"Thank you." Matt is not quite sure what will be revealed on the other side of the door. The new recruit enters the room followed by Viktor. "Oh God!" Matt whispers to himself.

He stares in shock at a huge underground hangar dug out of solid rock. The place is surrounded by metal scaffolding, and inside, are eight brownish saucer-shaped metallic aircraft under construction. They are sixty feet in diameter and look like a huge, squashed bells.

Viktor looks proudly at his creation. "This is the secret weapon that will win the war. They're the second Vril generation, called *Haunebu*."

Matt looks at him in amazement. "You have a previous generation before these?"

"Yes, we started the project nine years ago. We called the first generation RFZ discs."

"What happened to them?" Matt asks curiously.

"None of the original models remain. The aircraft were unstable due to mechanical unreliability and design flaws."

"I see."

"We solved most of the problems with the Haunebu's new design. The new aircraft are greatly improved."

As the two men walk down in the clandestine hangar, several people are busy working on the aircraft. Metal panels, which cover the hull, have been removed to allow access to the electromagnetic engines.

"How fast can they go?" Matt asks.

Viktor pauses for a second before replying. "With

the new, improved engine, we have been recording speed as high as nine thousand kilometers per hour."

Unsure if he had heard correctly, Matt asks, "Excuse me? Did you just say nine thousand kilometers per hour?"

"Yes! That's right," Viktor confirms.

"Sounds unbelievable." Matt has mixed feelings. He is both impressed and terrified by this number.

"Oh, believe me, that's just the beginning." Viktor stops in front of one of the Haunebus, which looks slightly different from the others and is a complete model. "This one is the second-generation Haunebu. It is modified and adapted to travel in space. Outside of earth's atmosphere, I believe the speed can be dramatically increased."

Matt looks at Viktor in disbelief. "How much faster?"

"Well, you will find that out for me. Congratulations, Mr. Müller. This is your first mission. Let me introduce you to your new *sturmbannführer.*"

Still surprised and somewhat confused at what Viktor has just told him, Matt continues to follow him under the Haunebu II's hull. They climb up using a ladder to reach the belly hatch. Inside the cabin, the setup is very different than a conventional aircraft and looks more like a primitive, miniature power station.

Matt sees Herbert in the pilot's seat reading a

document, while on the other side, Cedric is working on a section of the electrical power. The usual control yoke or stick system to fly the Haunebu II is replaced by some kind of lever.

Viktor walks up to Herbert and says, "Sturmbannführer Waizer, you have already met Hauptmann Müller."

Herbert turns and gives Matt a rather cold and unfriendly look.

"You will assist Mr. Waizer as his copilot for this first mission in space. If you succeed, you will make history," Viktor adds.

A woman scientist in her early thirties shows up from the floor hatch and interrupts Viktor. "Excuse me, Herr Doctor. We have an issue I would like you to take a look at."

"Yes, I'll be with you in just a second, Miss Orsic," Viktor says to her before finishing what he has to say to the new recruit. "Sturmbannführer Waizer will train you and explain your duty in preparation for the November 16 mission. So, if you would excuse me, I am needed elsewhere." And with that, Viktor exits the Haunebu II.

Matt takes a deep breath and turns to Herbert. "Listen, I apologize for this morning. I really didn't—"

Before Matt can finish his sentence, Herbert raises his hand and gestures for him to stop talking. "I have been forced to have a copilot for this mission without my consent. I need to make a few things clear. First, I do not like people who make me waste my time. Second, I do not like people who talk too much … And third, I do not need a new friend. Do I make myself clear?"

"Yes, sir," Matt says with mutual feelings toward his new supervisor.

"Good, let's get down to business," Herbert says before he continues. "I understand that Dr. Schauberger wants me to train you, but unfortunately, I don't have time to babysit. So—"

"I'll help him," Cedric quickly says, interrupting him. Waizer stares at Cedric for a moment with a cold face. "I'll take the responsibility to train him, and Dr. Schauberger doesn't have to know about it," he adds.

Herbert has a smirk on his face. "All right then, Mr. Heinrich. He's all yours." Herbert closes his manual and slaps it on Matt's chest. "Here, read this. You'll need to memorize it before we meet here tomorrow morning at the briefing. Six o'clock sharp. Don't be late."

"Yes, sir," Matt replies.

Herbert exits the Haunebu II hatch, which gives Matt and Cedric an opportunity to be alone for the first time. The concerned father, overwhelmed with emotions, approaches his son. The brief moment of silence speaks loudly of the intense emotions both men are experiencing as they try to hold back the tears.

Breaking the silence, Matt gently cries out, "Dad!"

"Matthew! But how … how did you manage to get here?"

Matt pulls up his left sleeve and shows his dad the time device. Cedric looks around through the portholes to be sure no one is watching and immediately pulls down Matt's sleeve to cover it. "You found the flash drive."

Matt simply nods his head.

"Oh my God, what have I done?" Cedric gasps. "I should have destroyed it."

"I'm glad you didn't, or else I wouldn't have been able to find you. I'm here to take you home," Matt says with conviction.

"Take me home? … Have you lost your mind? This is crazy. You should not be here, Son," Cedric says with a tone of fear in his voice.

"Dad! It's okay, everything is gonna be fine. I'm just glad I found you … Do you still have your time device?"

"No, all the electronics were fried, and I destroyed what was left of it six years ago. I didn't want that technology to fall in to the Nazi hands," Cedric says.

"Okay, then you take mine."

Matt pulls up his sleeve again, but before he can remove the time device, Cedric grabs his son's arm and stops him. "No, wait! I want you to hold on to it until

we find a safe way to get out of here. All right, Son?"
Cedric adamantly says.

Matt nods and changes the subject. "How did you
end up here?"

"I forgot to stop and smell the roses." Cedric
answered with a feeling of regret.

"What?" Matt asks, a bit confused by the answer.

"I was so obsessed with my work that I neglected
the repercussions of my achievement. It was too late
when I found out that the old Herbert Waizer had been
a Nazi and was up to no good."

"The family picture," Matt points out.

"Yeah, that one." Cedric goes on with the story:
"I caught Waizer using the time machine to send
documents filled with modern technologies back to
himself in this war time period. I can't stress enough
how devastating it would have been for our future if he
had succeeded. My options were limited, and the only
way I could stop him was to track down the time period
he had sent the information to. I was able to use the
gateway to retrieve the priceless package. I destroyed
it, but the unfortunate outcome was—"

"A one-way ticket," Matt says, finishing the sentence
for his dad. He rolls his eyes in disbelieve. "I don't know
which one I hate the most, the young Waizer or the old
Waizer. Both have tried to kill me already," he says
sarcastically, although he is truly irritated.

"What?" asks the concerned father.

Matt goes on with the discussion, ignoring his dad's reaction. "Why didn't you kill that son of a bitch when you got here?"

"I thought about it but then remembered that Waizer introduced me to your late mother," Cedric explains. "If he died—"

Once again, before he can finish the sentence, Matt interrupts. "I'll cease to exist."

"Most likely, and I'm not willing to take that chance."

Matt is looking through the porthole at another Haunebu under construction. The lower and higher magnetic Tesla coil motors are partially exposed. "What is your clearance level to access these saucers?"

"Full access … What do you have in mind?" Cedric asks.

"We have a time device, and I'm gonna need your help to open a gateway," Matt says.

Cedric scratches his head a bit confused. "I hate to say this, but I thought you knew that the time device you used to get here is only good for a one-way trip. I built a lot of those, and all of them burned."

"I know. I saw them at the lab, but mine is different. I have used it many times," Matt replies.

"How is that possible?" Cedric asks, completely baffled.

"You tell me, Dad. I used your blueprint to build the damn thing. I should be asking you this question."

"I don't know! That was not supposed to happen."

Matt puts his hand on the sleeve concealing the time device. "Trust me. This one will take us home," he insists.

Cedric nods. "Okay, but for now, I want to hear from you how you found me."

"It's been quite a bumpy ride," Matt says before giving Cedric the details of his latest adventure.

On the floor of the underground hangar, not too far away from Cedric and his son, Viktor is busy writing notes on a Haunebu blueprint.

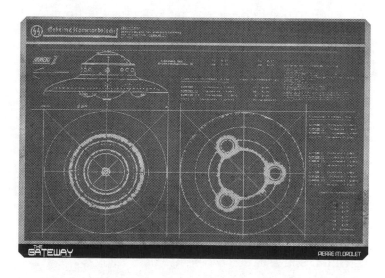

Viktor looks up for a second and sees Herbert walking up to him. "What do you think about your new copilot?" he asks.

"I don't like him," Herbert answers quickly before

adding, "There is something about Müller that just doesn't feel right, and he has a strange accent."

"You don't like anybody," Viktor says. He is not surprise by Herbert's reaction. "You didn't like your last copilot either."

"He was an idiot and got what he deserved," Herbert replies vehemently.

His last copilot had died in an explosion while testing the EMG (electro-magnetic-gravitic). The device is basically a small Tesla coil motor made especially for maintaining the earth's gravity in the Haunebu cabin in space. One Tesla coil is mounted under the floor, and the other one outside the cabin ceiling. Herbert blames his copilot for the disaster, saying that he pushed the g-force level too high and, as a consequence, overheated the power supply.

"Listen, I know you like to fly alone, but this mission requires two crew members. He is the best we can get who fits the profile that we need given the short notice … What do you have against him anyway?" Viktor asks.

Herbert has a smug look on his face. "Nothing … yet."

"I trust the judgment of General Becker, who recruited you as well, Herbert," Viktor says.

"General Becker has no idea what we're doing here. Why don't you invite him? I'm sure he'd be pleased to see those aircraft." Waizer says sarcastically while lighting up a cigarette.

As Herbert is walking away, the scientist just looks at him with an awkward smile before turning his attention back to the blueprint.

Matt removes one of the access panels from the floor of the cabin, exposing the lower Tesla coil motor. "How did you end up working on a time machine anyway?" he asks his dad.

Cedric already knows his son will not like the answer. "Based on Viktor's electromagnetic research, somehow the old Waizer saw the potential capabilities of Tesla coils to opening a gateway. A few years before you were born, he approached me with the theoretical idea of time travel and funded my own R & D department."

"Jesus! Him again," Matt exclaims. Just hearing the name *Waizer* triggers a strong repulsive reaction in him. "So, is it true? Is Viktor my grandfather?" he asks.

Feeling ashamed, Cedric nods. "So, the whole thing you told me about our family history is a lie?" Matt is getting upset as he continues to talk. "Why didn't you ever tell me that my grandfather was a Nazi?"

"I was going to tell you, but what was the point to bring up the subject when you had already decided to join the military and threw away a promising engineering career?" Cedric can't hide his disappointment and, in his defense, adds, "What good would it have done for you other than messing up your mind anyway?"

Although Matt understands his dad's point of view, for the first time, he doesn't feel the need for parental approval. "Dad, it was my choice to become a Marine pilot, not yours. As for our family history, I would rather have learned about it from you than from a conspiracy theory website … That is messed up."

Acknowledging his son's anger and disappointment, Cedric looks down without saying anything. Matt takes a deep breath and changes the subject to a more crucial issue at the moment.

"Well, Dad, better late than never. On a positive note, we finally get a chance to work together."

The last phrase brings a little smile to Cedric's face, as his son's acceptance and forgiveness of their family secret brings him some relief.

"Yeah, although not exactly the way I had originally imagine it," Cedric says.

"Me either … For the longest time, I thought you were dead, so I see this as a second chance for us. This means the world to me," Matt says before looking down at the access panel. "What is the maximum RPM of those Tesla coils?"

"About ten thousand." Cedric replied.

"Damn it! That's not enough," Matt says with frustration.

"I know, we need at least 20,000 RPM to open a gateway."

"Do you think you can do it?" Matt asks.

"Yes, I'll find a way," Cedric says, although he is worried about this difficult task. "I'm gonna need a lot of juice, and we'll have only one chance to make the trip."

"I know. Let's make it count," Matt adds with a smile.

Chapter 15

Bunker Next to the Airship Hangar

BACK IN HIS QUARTERS, HERBERT is smoking a cigarette while on the phone with a German officer at the Gestapo headquarters.

"Yes … Hans Müller. Send me his file immediately with anything you can find on him," Herbert says before hanging up the phone. His animosity toward the new recruit has developed into almost an obsession, so he initiates a covert investigation on him.

Underground Hangar

VIKTOR AND NINE OTHER SCIENTISTS, including Cedric, are gathered at a round-table meeting. Laid out on the table are multiple blueprints of the Haunebu II. Cedric takes the opportunity to discreetly pull Viktor aside for a private conversation.

After a long talk with Viktor, Cedric manages to

convince his father to let him conduct an experiment and test the effect on one of the Haunebus under construction. He sold the idea to Viktor that he could increase the power of the magnetic engine by reconfiguring the fixed magnets on the Tesla coils.

In spite of the fact that the majority of technicians are working on the space mission project, Viktor allows a small team to help his respected colleague with the experiment. Cedric first instructs the team to modify a section of the power supply adaptors on the generator. His task is to work on the fixed magnets on the Tesla coils.

This will be an intense and challenging week for both time travelers, and the most difficult undertaking is yet to come. Cedric has to modify the Tesla coil motor to a precise measurement/parameter in order to make it possible to open a gateway. Without the help of a computer, performing the calibration is like shooting at a target in the dark. To make things worse, there is no way to test it without attracting attention.

During the day, Matt is going through vigorous training for his space mission. The amount of information he has to learn in a short period of time is overwhelming. Amid all this, he is constantly seeking opportunities to spend some time with his dad in the Haunebu II cabin.

Cedric helps his son to become familiarized with the unconventional cockpit instruments and shows him how to operate the primitive, but efficient, navigation system. Herbert shows up once in awhile in the cabin by occupying himself with other Nazi scientists who are working on the control system.

One afternoon, Herbert brings the new recruit in a screening room to watch a few black-and-white documentary films on the early models of the RFZ disc crashes. The initial tests were conducted in a contained environment called a *flytrap*. It's an open circular base of an abandoned cooling tower, where a disc-shaped aircraft would be positioned in the middle and chained to the concrete columns surrounding it. One of the scenes shows the RFZ disc hovering low over the ground and then spinning out of control, before flipping upside down and crashing into the forest. Other footage shows a RFZ flying straight up into the sky and suddenly running out of power in midair. The disc-shaped aircraft falls from the sky like a brick before hitting the ground with tremendous destructive force.

Matt is not amused by all the crash scenes Waizer made him watch. It just adds more fuel to the fire for Matt's resentment toward him.

Bunker Next to the Airship Hangar

IN HIS OFFICE, VIKTOR WRITES the date November 9, 1944, on the back of a black-and-white photo, along with the names of all the people in the picture. This includes himself, Hans Müller, Stefan Heinrich, and Herbert Waizer. He puts the photo in a frame on the bookshelf.

As the evening approaches, Matt is alone in his quarters catching a breath as he reflects on all the work that still needs to be done and the various documents he has to review for his assignment. He is tired but can't sleep, because he has a lot on in his mind. Kayla's death is still vivid in his memory, and he can't stop worrying about what could possibly go wrong with the upcoming mission.

As for Herbert, he just received a folder with the name *Hans Müller* written on it. He reads through the files without paying any attention to the pictures inside, which works in Matt's favor. Much to his disappointment, there is no suspicious information against the new recruit.

Underground Hangar

THE DAY BEFORE THE MISSION, Matt feels more anxious than usual, and the lack of sleep is making it worse. Cedric has worked around-the-clock with his team. An external power generator is now in place behind the Haunebu under construction. High-voltage electrical cables are plugged in to the Haunebu's internal power supply.

Matt walks over his dad and helps him remove a

heavy metal panel from the power generator. "How are you doing, Dad?" Matt asks.

"I need more time," Cedric says with an agitated tone. "This is crazy! There is no way to know if a gateway will actually open. And even then, we will probably be shot before we can make the jump. This place is more secure than Fort Knox."

"Calm down, Dad! We'll find a way, and I'm gonna get you home." Matt looks at him with a comforting smile and adds, "Let's stick to the plan."

Cedric takes a deep breath and looks at his father, Viktor, walking down the aisle.

"Your grandfather has been asking a lot of questions," Cedric warns Matt. "I'm running out of justifications. I think he is getting suspicious of what I'm trying to do here."

There is a question that Matt has wanted to ask his dad but has not had the chance to bring up the subject until now. "You could have gone anywhere when you landed here. Why did you decide to come here and work for them?"

"I know what it looks like, Son, but I'm not working for the Nazis," Cedric says as he glances at Viktor. "I just wanted to be close to him and have an opportunity to—" He pauses for a moment without finishing his sentence. Cedric feels judged and uncomfortable talking about his father, but he decides to open up to his son. "He died when I was only a year old, and I never had the chance to get to know him. Viktor was the only family I had in this world before you arrived."

Matt can relate strongly to what his father is saying. He'd lost his mother in a car accident when he was still very young. "I'm sorry, Dad. I didn't mean—"

"It's all right, Son. You have the right to ask."

Matt looks at Viktor and has an awkward smile on his face. "Grandpa takes his Nazi shit very seriously … It's hard to believe that we're related to him."

"Tell me about it!" Cedric exclaims—"Your grandfather is not a bad man and remember that he doesn't have much choice but to cooperate with the Nazis. He is one of many brilliant German scientists who are forced to work for them under the close surveillance and control of the SS."

Matt looks at the Haunebu II. "Honestly, Dad, what are my chances of surviving this space mission?"

"If you were by yourself, I would say none. But you will be with Waizer, and obviously, he lives to become an old man. So, I would say you have a pretty good chance," Cedric says confidently.

The pep talk with his dad helps Matt to feel more at ease for the rest of the day.

Chapter 16

Airship Hangar
3:16 a.m.

UNDER A GIBBOUS MOON, THE Graf Zeppelin II is tied up to its anchor mast outside in the yard. A retractable portion of the floor inside the hangar is opened and reveals the subterranean Haunebu hangar below. The scaffolding has been removed around the Haunebu II. There is a lot of military activity in the airship hangar.

Underground Hangar

VIKTOR AND FIVE OF HIS colleagues, Cedric included, are inside the Haunebu II cabin for a last-minute inspection. Four cameras have been set up in front of the portholes. Matt takes a deep breath before taking his position in the copilot seat and buckles up. Herbert settles in to his side, seeming totally in control.

"Ready for takeoff, Herr Doctor," Herbert announces.

Viktor and his colleagues consult for a moment about technical details, and then all approve. The scientists salute the astronauts before exiting the cabin. Cedric looks pensive as he takes a last-minute look at his son.

Viktor turns his attention to both astronauts and says, "You are the pride of our nation. Good luck, gentlemen."

"Thank you, Herr Doctor," both men say.

Viktor exits and seals the hatch behind him. Herbert then takes command and starts up the magnetic engine, while Matt prepares for takeoff.

After a few seconds, the magnetic engine propulsion reaches an RPM fast enough for takeoff. A subtle reddish glow can be seen around the Haunebu's hull, and a pulsing strobe light is activated on top of the aircraft.

"Ready for liftoff," Herbert says.

Airship Hangar

VIKTOR, THE REST OF THE scientists, Cedric, and the soldiers watch proudly as the Haunebu II rises vertically in the air from the open floor of the airship hangar. The saucer-shaped aircraft then flies horizontally out of the hangar. A soldier films the historical event with a handheld black-and-white camera.

Herbert gives directives to his copilot. "EMG set the cabin's gravitational system to one G. We're going to make a forty-five degree climb."

Matt pushes on a small lever and turns the control wheel to the number one. "Done."

"On my mark, set the timer on the stopwatch for two minutes," Herbert says.

Matt sets the chronometer for two minutes. "Yes, sir. Ready when you are."

Herbert points the bow of the Haunebu II at the gibbous moon. "Liftoff!" he yells out.

Matt starts the countdown on the stopwatch as the pilot pushes forward on the control lever to increase power. The saucer accelerates rapidly into the dark sky. As their speed increases, the light around the Haunebu's hull changes from red to purple.

After only a few seconds, Matt looks at one of the

gauges, which indicates they have reached three thousand kilometers per hour. The Haunebu II continues to accelerate without creating any g-force effects on their bodies.

"Thirty seconds!" Matt calls out. He then conducts a routine check of the gauges on the control panel. "All instruments are okay," Matt confirms before looking back at the stopwatch. "One minute!"

Seconds seem to take forever as they prepare to leave the earth's atmosphere. "One minute, thirty!" Matt shivers from the roaring sounds and vibrations created by the high RPMs from the electromagnetic engine as they near the two-minute mark.

"Five, four, three, two, one. Stop!" Matt shouts out.

Herbert reduces the power to a minimum, and the saucer quickly comes to a stop. "What are your instruments showing?" he asks Matt.

"Anode and plasmode are okay; generator, temperature okay; oxygen, EMG, and cabin pressurization okay ... We're good," Matt answers.

The pilot turns the Haunebu II around so they can face earth. Matt looks out through the porthole with a smile at the beauty of the blue planet.

"Unbelievable!" he says in amazement as he takes in the breathtaking view of earth.

Herbert abruptly awakens Matt from his daydream. "Hey! Snap out of it. We have work to do," he says in a patronizing tone.

Both astronauts begin filming the orbital view of earth with the black-and-white camera.

After awhile, Herbert returns to the instrument panel. He removes a sextant and hands it to Matt. "Here, you know what to do. Leave the camera rolling."

"Yes, sir," Matt replies.

Herbert starts to slowly push forward on the throttle lever. He then looks at two navigational instruments, called *levy meisterkompass* and *peiltochterkompass*, which have replaced the compass to track their initial position in space. "The trajectory will be 0.586 mark 27.132," Herbert confirms.

"Got it!" Matt says.

He uses the sextant to get the coordinate location of their initial position from the Great Bear constellation and records it on his clipboard. He then returns to his seat and buckles up. Herbert looks irritated and comments, "We are in space. The harness is useless. Don't you know that?"

"Just a habit," Matt says.

Herbert rolls his eyes as he says, "On my mark, time three minutes on the stopwatch for the countdown."

Matt sets the chronometer and nods. The pilot pushes the throttle forward to the maximum RPM power.

"Now!" Waizer shouts out.

As Herbert pushes on the steering control, Matt starts the stopwatch. The Haunebu jumps out of the earth's orbit with an explosive acceleration. The copilot looks behind him to see earth getting smaller and smaller through the porthole.

"What do the instruments read?" Herbert asks.

"Everything is normal." Matt says while the roaring sounds and vibrations grow stronger. He turns back his attention to the stopwatch.

"One minute." The flying saucer keeps accelerating at an incredible speed. After covering a lot of space in a very short time, Matt calls out again, "Two minutes." As they near the last few seconds before the three-minutes mark on the stopwatch, the copilot begins to give the countdown. "Five, four, three, two, one. Stop!"

Herbert reduces the power to a minimum and stops the aircraft. Matt takes out the sextant and reads the coordinate location of their new position from the Great Bear constellation.

"That's unbelievable! I must have made a mistake," Matt says before recalculating.

"How fast?" Herbert asks.

"65,388 kilometers per hour," Matt replies.

"What? Let me see that." Herbert says, demanding to see the numbers.

He recalculates his copilot's math and arrives at the same result. "65,388 kilometers per hour! That's seven times faster than what we can do on earth." Waizer says in absolute astonishment.

"At this speed, we could reach the moon in less than six hours," Matt says.

"How would you know that?" Herbert asked in disbelieve.

Matt suddenly realized what he'd just said. There wouldn't be an accurate way to measure the distance from earth to the moon for another twenty years.

"That was just a rough guess," he quickly replies, hoping that Herbert wouldn't think too much of what he'd just said.

Herbert has an odd look on his face as he's trying to do the math himself. "Right," he says before giving his next order. "Set the stopwatch for two minutes, thirty seconds. We're heading back to earth."

"Done," Matt replies.

The pilot turns the bow of the Haunebu toward earth, pushes forward on the throttle to maximum power, and then pushes on the steering control one more time. "On my mark … now!" Herbert shouts out.

Ten seconds go by, and suddenly a warning sound goes off, as a red light on the cockpit instrument panel turns on. The EMG gauge shows an overheating problem. Matt stretches out his arm to grab the small lever to shut it down.

"Don't touch that!" Herbert yells out as he grabs his copilot by his left forearm. Unexpectedly, he feels the time device. Herbert quickly pulls back Matt's sleeve to expose what he felt. He sees the carbon-fiber cover of the mysterious object. "What is this?" he asks with an agitated voice, completely baffle.

Matt looks at Herbert without saying a word.

"Answer my question! What the hell is this thing?" the pilot asks again in a demanding, angry tone, expecting an explanation.

"Let go of my arm," Matt says with hostility, realizing his undercover identity has been exposed.

Herbert reaches for his holster and pulls out his Walther P38 pistol. Matt quickly reacts with his other hand by pushing the EMG lever to maximum power. The engine is already overheating and is close to a breaking point. Matt fights for his life against Herbert, who is trying to shoot him. He manages to make Herbert drop the pistol, but he is still harnessed to his seat and unable to move. Matt endures a few punches to his face as Herbert takes advantage of the situation.

The needle gauge on the EMG hits the critical red zone, and suddenly, an explosion under the cabin's floor shreds a section of the panel covers. Herbert is thrown up in the air and knocked unconscious. Weightlessness takes over the cabin, as the gravitational system is destroyed, and everything starts to float around them. Fortunately, the external hull of the Haunebu remains intact, but the cabin is severely damaged.

A warning alarm goes off when some debris from the

explosion make their way through the electromagnetic engine housing, causing severe power fluctuation. The saucer-shaped aircraft is out of control. Matt climbs out of his safety harness and makes his way to the pilot seat, where he struggles to shut down the power to stop the saucer.

"Come on! Come on!" he shouts out. The Haunebu is slowing down but still heading straight at the blue planet. Every second that goes by, the earth appears larger and larger. Fire ignites around the Haunebu's hull as it reenters earth's atmosphere and then turns into a fireball.

Matt pulls back on the steering stick and pushes the throttle lever in order to regain power. The Haunebu continues to fall from the sky like a fireball, out of control and at very high speeds.

"Come on!" Matt shouts out again, pleading with the aircraft as he tries to regain control.

Matt hears multiple clunking noises coming from under the cabin floor. He looks and sees small debris flying out of a shredded panel. As soon as the electromagnetic engine is clear from debris, Matt regains full control of the saucer and quickly changes his flight path angle to horizontal. He then pulls back on the throttle lever until the craft comes to an abrupt stop.

Matt drops his head on the control panel while he catches his breath from the chaos. The fire around the Haunebu's hull dissipates, and as he looks out through the portholes, Matt sees the face of the Statue of Liberty about a hundred feet away.

"I'm in New York!" he whispers.

Matt looks behind him and sees Herbert lying unconscious on the floor. He pulls out a Walther P38 pistol from his holster and walks up to Herbert. Matt aims the handgun at Herbert's head.

"The world would be a better place without you," Matt says as he pulls the trigger. Nothing happens. "Next time, I'll have a round in the chamber," he adds as he pulls back and releases the slide of his handgun.

Matt notices the sound of a distant airplane engine growing increasingly louder and louder. Through the portholes, he sees two Curtiss P-40 airplanes flying toward him in formation. Moments later, they open fire.

"Shit!" Matt yells out.

As fast as he can, Matt rips off some damaged electric cables hanging from the cabin ceiling and uses them to tie Herbert's wrists and ankles together before jumping in the pilot seat.

Both P-40 airplanes make their second approach and open fire again. Matt ducks, but the bullets are decelerating drastically when they hit the electromagnetic field of the saucer. The bullets bounce off the surface of the hull, causing minor damage. Without a second to spare, he quickly buckles up and takes control of the Haunebu. The saucer takes off in a fuming acceleration, leaving both P-40 fighter airplanes far behind.

Chapter 17

German Airspace
6:33 a.m.

THE HAUNEBU IS FLYING OVER the clouds. Matt is on his way back to Lake Constance but is still many miles away.

In the far distance, he catches a glimpse of what appear to be multiple black dots on the horizon. He slows down the engine to get a better visual but is moving too fast. Before he realizes what they are and is able to change course, the dots turn out to be a formation of seventy American B-17 Flying Fortress aircraft.

Right away, the gunners open fire at the saucer, and Matt sees tracer bullets coming toward the Haunebu. "No! No! That's not good," Matt shouts out.

As he flies through the B-17 battle formation, Matt pushes forward on the throttle lever and the steering control. Once again, the Haunebu flies off in a fast acceleration back to the base.

Airship Hangar

THE HAUNEBU MAKES ITS APPROACH and flies inside the airship hangar. Matt extracts the landing gear and lands the saucer before shutting down the engine. The military guards immediately close the huge doors of the hangar, and the area is quickly occupied with soldiers running to the saucer shaped aircraft. Matt rushes to Herbert, who is still unconscious, and pulls out a knife from his belt. He cuts the electric cables binding his hands and feet and checks for his pulse. A moment later, the hatch from the floor opens, and Viktor climbs in followed by Cedric. They both survey the wrecked cabin with disquietude.

"Dear Lord! What happened?" Viktor asks with concern.

"The EMG blew up," Matt says.

Viktor looks at Herbert, who is still motionless on the floor, and asks, "Is he alive?"

"Yes, but he needs medical attention."

Viktor yells through the hatch, "We need a medic right away!"

Viktor rushes to Herbert. A medic team quickly arrives and enters the cabin. Matt takes advantage of the momentary distraction with Herbert. He pulls Cedric aside, and they both walk to the hatch to exit the Haunebu.

"Listen," Matt begins. "I blew my cover with

Herbert, and on my way back here, I saw about seventy B-17 Bombers heading this way. We have to get out of here right now."

"Oh my God! I need more time," Cedric says as he stops for a moment and looks up through the Haunebu's portholes at Viktor.

Matt firmly grabs onto his father's shoulders and says, "We don't have any more time! It's over … We have to go now."

"It's too early … I told them I need another week," Cedric says.

Matt is puzzled. "What are you talking about, Dad?" Thinking for a second, he starts to connect the dots. "Do you have something to do with that oncoming air raid?"

Cedric nods. "I'm an American, Son. I told you I wasn't working for the damn Nazis. I'm here to make sure those saucers never go beyond the prototype stage."

A warm smile creeps across Matt's face. "That's my dad!" he says proudly.

Matt and Cedric are momentarily blinded by a camera flash. They look up to see that a photographer has just taken a picture of a group of soldiers standing nearby.

"Let's go home," Cedric says, and they briskly walk away from the hangar.

In the Haunebu, Viktor and the medic team are desperately trying to revive Herbert. After a few unsuccessful attempts, he finally wakes up and regains consciousness. Herbert glances around the cabin and abruptly asks, "Where is he?"

Viktor is confused by the odd question and just stares at Herbert for a moment.

Underground Hangar

MATT AND CEDRIC ARE WORKING on the external generator located behind the Haunebu under construction.

"Plug this one over there," Cedric says, pointing to the Haunebu's electric power supply located under the hull. "And bring me that power cable."

Cedric runs to a big electric box mounted on the wall and turns on all of the power switches. Suddenly, a loud alarm sound goes off.

"They know!" Cedric calls out.

He runs back to the external generator and turns on all the switches. Matt sees Herbert coming through the main door with Viktor and a group of soldiers.

"Damn it!" Matt exclaims.

Matt hides behind a wooden scaffolding as one soldier, who doesn't know what's going on, is walking toward him. He knocks out the soldier and hides the body, taking with him the machine gun and the extra magazines from the soldier's belt.

Herbert, Viktor, and the soldiers are walking in the aisle and getting closer to Matt's location. Herbert orders three soldiers to go check the area around the external generator where Cedric is hiding. As soon as the soldiers get close to the external generator, Matt jumps out and shoots them. Herbert and the other soldiers immediately open fire at Matt, blasting him with their machine guns. Matt takes cover as best he can.

Meanwhile, Herbert yells to the soldiers, "Cease fire! Can someone shut off that damn noise?!"

As soon as the alarm sound shuts off, Herbert turns his attention back to Matt. "Müller! You have nowhere to go. Surrender now!" he shouts.

Two soldiers walk to the area where Matt is taking cover. To slow them down, he shoots a few rounds at them, but the soldiers return fire. Herbert takes a grenade from a soldier's belt and throws it at Matt.

Matt sees the grenade falling not too far from him. "Fuck!" he cries out.

He manages to jump behind a big panel nearby to take cover. The explosion blast throws Matt and the metal panel against the scaffolding of a Haunebu.

Herbert gives his order to the soldiers. "You two, go get him and bring him back to me."

The two soldiers cautiously approach Matt, who is knocked out on the floor. They drag him back to Herbert, who fanatically lifts up Matt's shirtsleeve, expecting to find the device on his arm. Instead, he discovers it is gone. Herbert is furious and points his handgun at Matt's face.

"Where is that thing you had on your forearm?" Herbert asks indignantly.

Viktor steps forward and asks, "What thing?"

Matt looks at Herbert and says, "I don't know what you're talking about."

"I'll give you three seconds to answer me. Where is it?!" Herbert demands.

Matt remains silent, while Herbert pulls back the hammer of his handgun and aims at Matt's head. A loud voice echoes in the Haunebu's hangar.

"Waizer! Stop!" Cedric steps out from behind the external generator and shows himself. He is holding the time device in one hand and a grenade in the other. "If you shoot him, I will destroy it."

Herbert looks at Cedric for a brief moment and then points his handgun at him. "No, you won't," he says with a devious tone.

Without any warning, Herbert shoots Cedric in the stomach. Blood starts pouring down his lab coat as he falls to the floor unconscious. Herbert forgets about Matt for a moment and walks over to Cedric to get his hands on the mysterious device.

Before he can do so, the entire underground hangar begins to shake like an earthquake. Heavy dust and light fixtures from the ceiling start to fall all around them. Air raid sirens sound off, and everyone starts to run for their lives toward the exit door, including Viktor. Multiple explosions on the ground level seem to get closer and closer. Suddenly, one explosion destroys a section of the removable ceiling and falls into the hangar where the Haunebus are located. Twisted metal beams, concrete, and rubble of all kinds are falling to the ground.

Matt, who is still lying on the floor, looks up to the sky through the open ceiling to see what's going on. He can see B-17 Bombers dropping bombs as they fly through antiaircraft artillery explosions. "Here comes the cavalry," Matt says to himself.

Outside the base, bombs are exploding on the ground all over the place. One bomb hits the tail of the LZ-130 Hindenburg and blasts it into flames. The gray skin surface on the airship quickly burns, exposing the massive aluminum skeleton frame underneath. It collapses to the ground in a twisted, metal wreck.

Inside the underground hangar, Matt stands up from the wreckage and runs as fast as he can to Cedric. "Dad! Dad!" he cries out.

Cedric wakes up and looks at his son. "Matthew … do you hear that?"

"Hear what?" Matt asks painfully.

Cedric turns his head and looks at the external generator. He can hear the electric crackling noise.

"That's the sound of your exit ticket," he says before giving his son the time device. "It's already set."

"No way. I didn't come this far to leave without you! Get up, Dad!" Matt tries to pick him up.

Cedric is losing a lot of blood and starts to look pale. "Matthew, stop! Take it! It's over for me ... Please forgive me for what I've put you through. I'm so proud of you and the man you've become ... Go ... go before it's too late. I love you, Son," Cedric says with his last breath.

Matt watches helplessly as his dad peacefully closes his eyes. Tears of sadness and anguish flood Matt's eyes. "Dad! Dad! Oh God no! I love you too. Dad ... Good-bye." Sill holding his dad in his arms, Matt gives him a final kiss on the forehead before gently laying him down.

He then rushes under the Haunebu and grabs the ladder. Midway into the hatch, Matt hears a gunshot and then feels it pierce his forearm.

The time device has been hit. Blood and carbon-fiber fragments splatter around him. Herbert is still on his knees and covered with dust from the wreckage.

"Where are you going, Hans?" Herbert says amid the chaos.

Herbert fires two more rounds at Matt before his gun jams. Painfully, Matt continues to climb up the ladder into the cabin of the aircraft and closes the hatch behind him. In a last minute frantic rage, Herbert throws his handgun and looks around to see if he can find another weapon.

Inside the Haunebu's cabin, the floor and ceiling are stripped of metal panels, and both of the giant Tesla coil motors are exposed. Matt walks carefully on the metal frame to the instrument panel to power up the electrical system.

Outside the Haunebu, Herbert picks up a machine gun from the debris. As he stares at Matt through one of the portholes, he asks with a harsh tone of voice, "What are you doing up there?" Frustrated, Herbert opens fire at the cabin's external wall paneling.

Matt flinches when one of the bullets hit a porthole glass right in front of him. In a scurry, he pushes forward on the throttle lever at full power. Both Tesla coils start to spin in opposite directions, rapidly increasing speed. Because there is no metal plating to shield the cabin, electrical sparks and blue static electricity are flying all over the place with a thunderous crackling sound.

Matt turns on the time device, but it is malfunctioning. Half of the screen display shows white noise and interference. Amid the chaos, he's struggling to hang on to a metal handle bolted on the cabin's wall to avoid getting sucked in to the electrical storm that's been generated by the howling wind vortex and the magnetic energy.

Herbert climbs on the scaffolding next to the Haunebu and fires multiple rounds at the porthole glass, but the magnetic field impedes the bullets from penetrating. In a desperate attempt to get Matt, the frustrated Nazi jumps through the magnetic field and lands hard on the saucer rim.

Inside the cabin, all hell is breaking loose around Matt as he frantically tries to make the time device work. "Come on! Come on!" he shouts out in desperation.

There's smoke coming from the vent of the overheated external electrical generator, and the heavy-duty power cables have spontaneously caught on fire.

Meanwhile, Herbert stands up on the external saucer hull and looks through one of the portholes. "Hans! You're a dead man!" he yells out like a madman.

Herbert takes his machine gun and fires into the porthole glass until it shatters. Suddenly, from the center of the raging electrical storm, an eerie blue spark forms in the air, and a single electrical discharge hits and shuts down the time device.

"Noooo!" Matt cries out before looking over at Herbert. He then looks back at the raging gateway, knowing this is the end. His last thoughts are of the three people he loves the most—Kayla, Cedric, and Daniel.

"I'm sorry," he humbly whispers to himself before letting go of his grip on the metal handle. The time traveler is violently sucked into the gateway and vanishes in a big bang.

Herbert is thrown into the air from the powerful aftermath shock wave generated by the unstable gateway and falls on some rubble from the bombing. With eyes wide open, the Nazi pilot is lying on his back in shock as he tries to wrap his brain around what he had just witnessed.

Chapter 18

Inside the Gateway

THE GATEWAY OPENS UP IN the sky with electric discharges flying from the center, ejecting Matt in a free fall.

The time traveler screams in a state of panic and ends up plunging headfirst into a large pool of water. Something inexplicable happens while he is submerged underwater, which seems to defy the law of physics. Instead of swimming back up to the surface, Matt finds himself going deeper as he heads toward a light coming from the bottom of the pool. Once he finally reaches the light and strangely surfaces, he is able to catch his breath.

While floating in the water and resting from his turbulent trip, Matt looks around and sees a beautiful flower garden with tall trees surrounding the huge pool of water. Everything is dreamlike and seems to be glowing with light. Matt notices the water around his arm has a reddish tinge of blood.

"Great! Just what I need," Matt says to himself.

Exhausted and injured, Matt swims out of the pool and removes the time device from his forearm. He then tears a strip of cloth from the bottom of his shirt and wraps it tightly around his wounded arm.

"Damn it!" he shouts out in pain.

With the pain intensifying, Matt's exhaustion kicks in deeper, leading him lie down on his back for a brief rest.

As Matt turns his head to the side, he can't believe his eyes. Sitting before him is what appears to be the office chair that the old Waizer had thrown into the gateway. Now more alert, Matt starts to look around.

Above the tree line, he spots two large griffin statues, as large as the sphinx, sitting side by side. Behind the two statues is an oasis filled with lush greenery and waterfalls. In the near distance, he sees an enormous step pyramid. The whole landscape looks like a gigantic sand mandala coming to life.

"Where the hell am I?" Matt asks himself in fascination.

A gentle male voice startles Matt. "Very beautiful, isn't it?" the mysterious man says.

An old monk walks up to Matt and smiles at him.

"Yeah," Matt answers.

"You look terrible. Playing with energies beyond comprehension is not safe and disturbs one's peace," the old monk says.

Matt is not in the mood for a lecture. "I'm sorry. Who … who are you?"

The old man looks around and takes a deep breath. "Oh … I have been called many names. I am usually referred to the guardian, but today you can call me Bob."

"Well, Bob. What is this place, and what am I doing here?" Matt asks.

The old monk looks at him with a straight face. "This is heaven, and you are dead," He says in a matter-of-fact tone.

Matt suddenly looks worried, but the old man starts to laugh.

"No, I am just kidding. You are not dead, and this place is the manifest apotheosis of impermanence." The monk reaches out and gives Matt a hand.

"You're killing me, Bob!" Matt says, still perplexed about who he is talking with and where he has landed. The time traveler welcomes the monk's gesture to help him and stands up.

"We don't have too many visitors." Bob says.

"I bet," Matt says as he looks around. "I'm still in the gateway … Aren't I?"

The old man smiles at him and comments, "Ahhh, very perceptive of you."

Beginning to realize the gravity of his situation, Matt looks at the damaged time device. "I have nothing left, and I'm stuck here … great! Everything is just getting better and better." He looks at the old man and smiles back at him. "Okay, Bob, I give up! So, what now?"

The old monk begins to approach Matt as a sudden, swirling wind rises. "The universe works in mysterious ways. In essence, free will brought you here. Despite your occasional recklessness and lack of humility, you ultimately have a pure heart with good intentions, which will help you stay clear at critical moments in life. Now, I would like to offer you some guidance."

"What do you mean? What kind of guidance?" Matt asks, a bit surprised.

"Simple. The next decision you will make is very important. Be mindful and choose your words wisely."

Matt wishes he had heard these words of caution

from the monk before his journey through time had started. The advice seems to be coming too late given his present situation. "I'm sorry," he says. "I don't understand the meaning of all this."

"You will," the monk says with a mystical smile. "You have a second chance, so please don't come back here. You go now. Bye! ... Bye!"

The swirling wind grows stronger. Matt looks around and sees the landscape starting to disintegrate into a sandstorm.

"What? Hey!" Matt is desperate to get more information from the monk. "Wait a min—"Before he can finish his sentence, the guardian swiftly but gently pushes on Matt's chest. Suddenly, the time traveler feels an incredible acceleration, as if he were launched backward out of a cannon. In an instant, everything becomes blindly bright.

Chapter 19

OUT OF NOWHERE, THE TIME traveler reappears as he leaps out from sparks of light and lands on a concrete floor. Matt is disoriented and nauseated from the travel. He looks down at his feet and sees a yellow X marked with duct tape.

"Is everything all right, Matthew?" a familiar voice asks.

As soon as he hears the old man, Matt has a strange feeling of déjà vu.

"Yes … yes, I think so," he says as he looks around and realizes he is back in Waizer's lab. The monk had sent him to the moment he'd returned from his first time-travel experiment. Matt's mind is racing—he realizes he is about to reveal to Herbert and Karl Waizer who would win the presidential election.

Matt is no longer wearing a Nazi uniform and is instead in his regular clothes. Herbert and Karl are standing a few feet in front of him. "How long have I been gone?" the time traveler asks.

"For us, it's been no less than three minutes," Herbert says. "How was it for you?"

"Never mind. I was just wonder—"

Herbert interrupts Matt before he can finish his sentence. "Do you have the answer to my question?"

Anxiously awaiting the news, Karl jumps in. "Am I going to be the next president of the United States?"

Matt looks at both men. Recalling his conversation with the monk, this time, he remembers to choose his words carefully. Taking a deep breath, he extends a handshake to Karl. "Congratulations, Mr. President."

Karl is obviously delighted. "Yes!"

He takes a firm grip of Matt's hand and gives him a handshake. Karl then turns to his father to give him a hug.

"That's my boy!" Herbert says to his son with his usual smirk. "Or should I say … Mr. President."

"If you'll excuse me, I'm sure you two want some time alone to celebrate your victory," Matt interjects. "I'm going to take the device into the safe."

As Matt starts to walk away, Herbert calls out to him. "Matthew!"

"Yes, Mr. Waizer?"

"Thank you … Your father would be very proud of you," Herbert says.

Matt nods before walking away with a subtle, satisfied smile on his face. As soon as he's alone and out of sight, he removes the time device from his forearm. Matt grabs firmly on to the device and forcefully twists it until it snaps. On the broken glass display, a blue screen with error codes can be seen for a few seconds before it shuts down.

Brentwood, Los Angeles

MATT RUSHES IN THE HOUSE while sending a quick text message on his smartphone. He is calling out as he runs. "Kayla!"

Nobody answered.

He stops in the living room and looks through the glass patio door, where he sees his sweetheart watering the garden in the backyard. Matt instantly experiences a deep sense of relief and happiness, as if he has been given a second chance. He opens the patio door and walks up to her.

Kayla turns around and sees her love. "Wow! You're home early," she says.

Without saying a word, Matt gently takes Kayla in his arms and holds her for a while. He gives her a soft kiss—two lovers reunited after being separated for a lifetime.

Kayla feels something is different about him. "Wow! What was that?" she questions. A bit confused, she looks at Matt and adds, "Is everything all right?"

Matt smiles at her. "Yes … Yes, it is now."

The couple sits down on the patio, and Matt tells her the whole story, starting with his first meeting with Herbert Waizer. At first, it sounds too incredible to be true, but Kayla knows he couldn't have made up something as far-fetched with such vivid detail. When Matt is done telling his story, Kayla is more understanding than he had anticipated.

Matt reflects on his experience for a moment before adding, "Time travel is a seductive idea, but in reality, it's a powerful technology that we are not yet ready to handle. It should be left alone. I used it with only good intentions, and look what happened—I got you, Dan, and my dad killed."

As Kayla reflects on what she's just heard, she realizes that an important detail of the story doesn't add up. Kayla finds herself stuck in the midst of a catch-22.

"Let me get this straight. Tonight, you're supposed to travel in the future and then go back in the past to Nazi Germany." As Kayla speaks, she pauses to think about the mind-boggling information for a moment. "But now all that has changed, and you are not going anymore … So, how can you be with your dad and your grandfather in a picture from 1944?"

A chilling sensation goes through Matt's back. "You're right!" he answers anxiously.

Someone is ringing the doorbell.

Kayla gives him a puzzled look for a moment and says. "I'll get the door."

Kayla goes to the front door while Matt runs to the garage. He immediately grabs the box labeled *Cedric Schauberger*. As he flips the box upside down, a pile of pictures falls out on the floor. He looks through the pictures and finds the one he is looking for.

"The family picture," Matt whispers.

Kayla and Daniel walk in the garage.

"I got your text. So what's up?" Daniel asks.

Matt takes the black-and-white photo and stares at it for a moment. Viktor, Cedric, and Herbert are still in the picture, but to his amazement, he is not there anymore. He gives Kayla the photo to see for herself.

She looks at Matt for some answers. "What does this mean?" she asks.

"This means I must have created a paradox," Matt says.

"Is that bad?" Kayla asks, clearly a bit concerned.

"I don't know, but I still have to take care of some unfinished business with a Nazi," Matt says.

Daniel is confused and has no idea what they're talking about. "What did I miss?"

Epilogue

Northridge, WTRD
Three Days Later, Election Night

IN HIS OFFICE, HERBERT IS paying close attention to the news coverage playing on his television. The anchorman is reporting in front of a digital US map, which shows the fifty states colorized as red or blue.

"We have the final result of the election, and Andrew Cooper is officially the new president-elect of the United States," the anchorman announces. "A few minutes ago, Karl Waizer issued his concession speech."

Herbert is enraged when he sees Andrew Cooper celebrating his victory as the new president.

Meanwhile, Matt is back in the lab at Waizer Corporation. He takes out the C-4 plastic explosive devices from his backpack and rigs the lab with timed explosives. Before he leaves, Matt sets off the fire alarm system and throws a few smoke grenades in the corridor. The deafening alarm noise sets off a panic, and the entire staff frantically rush for the building's exits.

Back in Herbert's office, the old man's rage triggers a long-forgotten memory of a traumatic encounter he'd had back in Nazi Germany with a man named Hans Müller. It had been a shock for Herbert at the time, as he'd witnessed and recognized the man as Matthew seemingly vanish into thin air. And then there was the aftermath—a horrific blast of sparks and powerful shockwave. This traumatic thought creates so much stress for Herbert's psyche that it triggers a violent heart attack. As both his mind and his heart are overcome, the old man's body falls lifelessly to the floor.

At the same moment, Matt is riding his motorcycle out of the WTRD facility. He is on his way to meet up with his sweetheart and best friend, who are waiting for him on the side of the road.

Once Matt is safely outside the Waizer complex, and reunited with Kayla and Daniel, he takes out his smartphone and a detonator from his jacket. Using his phone, he sends an email to multiple news stations; attached is the black-and-white family picture along with information about the Nazi officer.

PIERRE M. DROLET

"That will take care of Karl's political agenda," Matt says before turning his attention to the detonator. "Herbert Waizer once told me that a certain section of the facility didn't officially exist." He presses the detonator's button before finishing his thought. "Now it's for real."

From the road, they can see the lab blow up in a big, devastating explosion. As he watches the smoke billow into the sky, Matt assumes all of the time machine equipment being destroyed by the flames.

"So, what now?" Kayla asks.

Matt reaches into his pocket and retrieves his father's USB drive. "There's a storm coming, and we need to be prepared."

"What are you gonna do with that?" Daniel asks, looking at the flash drive.

Matt glances at Kayla for her advice.

"This is your dad's legacy. I would hold on to it for a while. Besides, you wouldn't have found your way back to me without it," she says with a smile as she puts on her helmet.

Matt ponders Kayla's words for a moment and then puts the USB drive back in his pocket. With the tiny device tucked safely away, Matt, Kayla, and Daniel start their motorcycle engines and ride away.

The End

Glossary

For more information, here some keywords you can use to look it up online.

Bombers B-17 Fortress

(wikipedia) The Boeing B-17 Flying Fortress is a four-engine <u>heavy bomber</u> aircraft developed in the 1930s for the <u>United States Army Air Corps</u> (USAAC). Competing against <u>Douglas</u> and <u>Martin</u> for a contract to build 200 bombers, the <u>Boeing</u> entry outperformed both competitors and more than met the Air Corps' expectations. Although Boeing lost the contract because the prototype crashed, the Air Corps was so impressed with Boeing's design that they ordered 13 more B-17s for further evaluation. From its introduction in 1938, the B-17 Flying Fortress evolved through numerous <u>design advances</u>.

Curtiss P-40 aircraft

(wikipedia) The Curtiss P-40 Warhawk was an American single-engined, single-seat, all-metal fighter and ground-attack aircraft that first flew in 1938. The P-40 design was a modification of the previous Curtiss P-36 Hawk which reduced development time and enabled a rapid entry into production and operational service. The Warhawk was used by most Allied powers during World War II, and remained in frontline service until the end of the war. It was the third most-produced American fighter, after the P-51 and P-47; by November 1944, when production of the P-40 ceased, 13,738 had been built, all at Curtiss-Wright Corporation's main production facilities at Buffalo, New York.

Fly Trap or the Henge

(wikipedia) Based upon certain external indications, Witkowski states that the ruins of a metal framework in the vicinity of the Wenceslas mine (aesthetically dubbed "The Henge"), may have once served as a test rig for an experiment in "anti-gravity propulsion" generated with *Die Glocke*; others, however, dismiss the derelict structure as simply being a conventional industrial cooling tower.

Foo fighter

(wikipedia) This is a term used by <u>Allied</u> <u>aircraft</u> <u>pilots</u> in <u>World War II</u> to describe various <u>UFOs</u> or mysterious aerial <u>phenomena</u> seen in the skies over both the <u>European</u> and <u>Pacific Theater of Operations</u>.

F-35 Lightning II

(wikipedia) The Lockheed Martin F-35 Lightning II is a family of single-seat, single-engine, <u>fifth-generation</u> <u>multirole fighters</u> under development to perform <u>ground attack</u>, <u>reconnaissance</u>, and <u>air defense</u> missions with <u>stealth</u> capability. The F-35 has three main models; the F-35A is a <u>conventional takeoff and landing</u> variant, the F-35B is a <u>short take-off and vertical-landing</u> variant, and the F-35C is a <u>carrier-based</u> variant.

Haunebu

(wikipedia) In <u>UFOlogy</u>, <u>conspiracy theory</u>, <u>science fiction</u>, and <u>comic book</u> stories, claims or stories have circulated linking <u>UFOs</u> to <u>Nazi Germany</u>. The German UFO theories describe supposedly successful attempts to develop advanced aircraft or spacecraft prior to and during <u>World War II</u>, and further assert the post-war survival of these craft in secret underground bases in <u>Antarctica</u>, South America or the United States, along with their creators. According to the limited available information on the UFOs, various potential code-names or sub-classifications of Nazi UFO craft such as *Rundflugzeug, Feuerball, Diskus, Haunebu, Hauneburg-Geräte, V7, Vril, Kugelblitz* (not related to the self-propelled anti-aircraft gun of the same name), *Andromeda-Geräte, Flugkreisel, Kugelwaffen*, and *Reichsflugscheiben* have all been referenced.

Mandala

(wikipedia) The mandala can be shown to represent in visual form the core essence of the Vajrayana teachings. The mind is "a microcosm representing various divine powers at work in the universe." The mandala represents the nature of experience, and the intricacies of both the enlightened and confused mind.

Maria Orsic or (Maria Orsitsch)

(wikipedia) Maria Orsitsch was the head of the 'The All German Society for Metaphysics' (Alldeutsche Gesellschaft für Metaphysik) founded in the early 20th century as a female circle of mediums who were involved in extraterrestrial telepathic contact. The society was later renamed the 'Vril Society' or 'Society of Vrilerinnen Women'. In 1917 Maria Orsitsch is said to have made contact with extraterrestrials from Aldebaran with her female Vril circle. Later in 1919 the Vril circle met with other groups in a small forester's lodge in the vicinity of Berchtesgaden to discuss a possible voyage to Aldebaran to meet the Aliens by the construction of Nazi UFOs. Notes on this space mission are discussed in a recent detailed analysis of Nazi Occultism entitled *Black Sun: Aryan Cults, Esoteric Nazism, and the Politics of Identity.*

Me 262 aircraft

(wikipedia) The Messerschmitt Me 262 *Schwalbe* (English: "Swallow") of Nazi Germany was the world's first operational jet-powered fighter aircraft.[5] Design work started before World War II began, but engine problems and top-level interference prevented the aircraft from attaining operational status with the Luftwaffe until mid-1944. Compared with Allied fighters of its day, including the British jet-powered Gloster Meteor, it was much faster and better armed.[6] One of the most advanced aviation designs in operational use during World War II,[7] the Me 262 was used in a variety of roles, including light bomber, reconnaissance and even experimental night fighter versions.

Meisterkompass and Peiltochterkompass

Additionally normal navigation systems referring somehow to magnetic fields were completely useless and a special, magnetic independent navigation instrumentation designed, the celestial guidance system.

Operation Paperclip

(wikipedia) Operation Paperclip was the <u>Office of Strategic Services</u> (OSS) program used to recruit the scientists of <u>Nazi Germany</u> for employment by the United States in the aftermath of <u>World War II</u>. It was conducted by the <u>Joint Intelligence Objectives Agency</u> (JIOA), and in the context of the burgeoning <u>Cold War,</u> one purpose of Operation Paperclip was to deny German scientific expertise and knowledge to the <u>Soviet Union</u> and the <u>United Kingdom,</u> as well as inhibiting <u>post-war Germany</u> from redeveloping its military research capabilities.

RFZ disc

(discaircraft.greyfalcon) The series began with the RFZ-1 which was constructed after the Vril Gesellschaft had purchased the fallow land surrounding the Arado Brandenburg aircraft plant for future flight testing. The RFZ-1 took to the air in 1937 on its first and only flight at Arado Brandenburg. The record of this historic flight did not end in success.

Spitfire aircraft

(wikipedia) The Supermarine Spitfire is a British single-seat <u>fighter aircraft</u> that was used by the <u>Royal Air Force</u> and many other <u>Allied</u> countries during and after the <u>Second World War</u>. The Spitfire was built in many variants, using several wing configurations, and was produced in greater numbers than any other British aircraft. It was also the only British fighter to be in continuous production throughout the war. The Spitfire continues to be a popular aircraft, with approximately <u>50 Spitfires</u> being airworthy, while many more are static exhibits in aviation museums all over the world.

Viktor Schauberger

(wikipedia) Viktor Schauberger (30 June 1885, Holzschlag, <u>Upper Austria</u> – 25 September 1958, <u>Linz,</u> Austria) was an Austrian forest caretaker, <u>naturalist,</u> <u>philosopher</u>, <u>inventor</u> and <u>biomimicry</u> experimenter.

Schauberger developed his own ideas based on what he observed in nature. In *Implosion* magazine, a magazine released by Schauberger's family, he said that aeronautical and marine engineers had incorrectly designed the propeller. He stated:

"As best demonstrated by Nature in the case of the aerofoil maple-seed, today's propeller is a pressure-screw and therefore a braking screw, whose purpose is to allow the heavy maple-seed to fall parachute-like slowly towards the ground and to be carried away sideways by the wind in the process. No bird has such a whirling thing on its head, nor a fish on its tail.

Only man made use of this natural brake-screw for forward propulsion. As the propeller rotates, so does the resistance rise by the square of the rotational velocity. This is also a sign that this supposed propulsive device is unnaturally constructed and therefore out of place.

(cosmicpolymath) One of his more esoteric projects occurred In the middle of the WWII when he was working under the close surveillance and control of SS troops in Nazi Germany, on a project which saw him designing an anti-gravity motor for a prototype "flying saucer" know as the Vril. Viktor was forced to work for the Nazis in the Mauthausen concentration camp, with the threat of death an ever present reality. The Nazis focused only on the possible military application of his ideas. The unscrupulous actions of first, Nazi Germany then Soviet Russia and eventually Cold War America to use his inventions for their own selfish purposes, completely ruined and finally destroyed his life.

Vril energy /Vril generator/Vril Society

(wikipedia) Publications on the Vril Society in German

The book of <u>Jacques Bergier</u> and <u>Louis Pauwels</u> was published in German with the title: *Aufbruch ins dritte Jahrtausend: von der Zukunft der phantastischen Vernunft* (literally *Departure into the Third Millennium: The Future of the Fantastic Reason*) in 1969.

In his book *Black Sun*, Professor Nicholas Goodrick-Clarke refers to the research of the German author Peter Bahn. Bahn writes in his 1996 essay, "Das Geheimnis der Vril-Energie" ("The Secret of Vril Energy"),[16] of his discovery of an obscure esoteric group calling itself the "Reichsarbeitsgemeinschaft", which revealed itself in a rare 1930 publication *Vril. Die Kosmische Urkraft* (Vril, the cosmic elementary power) written by a member of this Berlin-based group, under the pseudonym "Johannes Täufer" (German: "John [the] Baptist"). Published by the influential astrological publisher, Otto Wilhelm Barth (whom Bahn believes was "Täufer"), the 60-page pamphlet says little of the group other than that it was founded in 1925 to study the uses of Vril energy. The German historian Julian Strube has argued that the historical existence of the "Reichsarbeitsgemeinschaft" can be regarded as irrelevant to the post-war invention of the Vril Society, as Pauwels and Bergier have developed their ideas without any knowledge of that actual association. Strube has also shown that the Vril force has been irrelevant to the other members of the "Reichsarbeitsgemeinschaft," who were supporters of the theories of the Austrian inventor Karl Schappeller (1875–1947).